Hellkite

Geraldine Mills

HELLKITE

Hellkite

is published in 2014 by
ARLEN HOUSE
42 Grange Abbey Road
Baldoyle
Dublin 13
Ireland
Phone: +353 86 8207617
Email: arlenhouse@gmail.com
www.arlenhouse.blogspot.com

978–1–85132–100–1, paperback
978–1–85132–101–8, hardback limited edition

International distribution by
SYRACUSE UNIVERSITY PRESS
621 Skytop Road, Suite 110
Syracuse, New York
USA 13244–5290
Phone: 315–443–5534/Fax: 315–443–5545
Email: supress@syr.edu
www.syracuseuniversitypress.syr.edu

Typesetting by Arlen House
Printed in Ireland by Brunswick Press
Cover Artwork:
'Death in Florence'
by Pauline Bewick

Contents

7 *Acknowledgements*

13 Centre of a Small Hell

27 This Street with Looking-Glass Eyes

35 Frost Heave

45 Drinking his Strength Back

53 The Devil's Dye

57 The Best Man for the Job

67 The Call

77 Hellkite

87 Every Piece of Ivory a Dead Elephant

95 Apidea

105 Backmasking

117 Foraging

127 Once Bitten

139 Pretty Bird, Why You So Sad?

147 Feeding the Wolf of Lies

160 *About the Author*

ACKNOWLEDGEMENTS

Thanks are due to the editors of the following journals in which versions of these stories first appeared: *Willesden Herald New Short Stories 6, Crannóg, RTÉ Guide, South of the County: New Myths and Tales, The Clifden Anthology, Galway Stories, Celebrating What Truly Matters, Ireland's Own*.

'Centre of a Small Hell' and 'This Street with Looking-Glass Eyes' were broadcast in the Francis MacManus Short Story Competitions, 2009 and 2011.

Special thanks to all at the Talking Stick and Saturday Peers where many of these stories got their first outing.

My deepest gratitude to Alan Hayes of Arlen House for his constant dedication, support and endless capacity to produce first-class books.

My gratitude to Galway County Council for their Individual Artist Award and bursary to the Tyrone Guthrie Centre where this collection was completed.

For Peter

Hellkite

Centre of a Small Hell

The morning after his wife's ashes were brought back home, Bernard Curran took a sledgehammer to the hunting table out there in the yard where the air was still enough for snow. He grabbed the end of it and dragged it across the stone tiles, the door slammed behind him and the commotion woke the house. Keeper started barking.

Hansie was down the stairs first because that's where she spent the night, asleep on the third step, refusing to budge when her father didn't come back from the fields. Carmel was fast after her.

The weather hit Bernard as soon as he touched outside. The children came out after him, crying as the cold came up through the soles of their feet. Colder than the day before, and the pain sliced across his forehead. He shouted at them to stay back so they stood some distance from his rage, shivering. He swung the hammer in an arc above his shoulder and brought it crashing down. Keeper whined, straining at the bit of baling twine that Bernard had tied him with to the barn door. He took no notice of them as the hammerhead struck the beautiful wood, gouged into its sheen.

Then he struck it again.

The day before he had stood at the train station, sleet hitting off the shoulders of his coat as his daughters in heavy duffels and wool hats hunched beside him.

February and a flurry of wind whipped around their ankles. A sprinkling of wet snow settled in the corners of the platform as if it were a white bird moulting. Mrs Purdis had advised Bernard of their arrival in a telegram four days before. She told them that they would know her by her black hat with the red rose on it and by the wooden box she carried.

The train pulled into the station, the heavy-set woman heaped herself down the steps and across the platform, the rose on the side of her hat not so much a rose as a red wound, opening up.

'Mr Curran?'

Bernard looked down at the small, round woman, her face flabby and strained from too much sherry and sweetmeats.

'Yes', he said.

'Well then, that wasn't too difficult, now was it?'

Bernard took the box, the dark, wooden box, with his wife's ashes in it from Mrs Purdis and passed it to his daughter Carmel. The woman, whose voice sounded like a lifetime of someone living off other people's endeavours, continued.

'And who are you?', she said, peering down at the two girls. Then she pronounced their names to the whole station: Carmel, Hansie, shaking their hands one by one.

'She is all yours now', she said.

Bernard could feel Carmel's body shaking more from what she held than the cold all around her. He didn't feel far off it himself. Mrs Purdis turned, straightened her hat, pinched Hansie's cheek as she stepped back into her carriage and the stationmaster gave the signal for the train to pull away.

His younger daughter stood beside him and went to put her small hand into his. Bernard pulled from her as if he had been scalded, turned. Then, followed by his two children, he hurried out of the station. He didn't stop to greet anyone, even his neighbour Tom Mahangy who had come to collect a sack of cattle feed. He left Tom standing, scratching his head, opening and closing his mouth like a small bird.

Bernard rushed towards the car. The children half-ran, half-walked after him trying to keep up. Snow had gathered along the edges of the windows, around the mirrors of the blue Anglia, and slid back off the boot as Bernard opened it for no reason and closed it again on the bags of cement, old bicycle tyres and a pickaxe that needed a new handle.

'Sit in there', he said, to Carmel pointing to the front seat and moved a bundle of old coats aside. Hansie got in the back. Then he sat in himself. The door was stiff so he had to open it wide again, letting the cold air in on top of them, and pulling it with force until it closed. He wound down the window and waved his hand through as he pulled out into the road for home.

He looked across at Carmel in the seat beside him, the wooden box on her lap. They drove along roads lined by fields marked out with stonewalls, snow secreted in pockets along them, grass hidden by white, trees by the edges dark as thunder.

It had come to this.

He waited for the house to come to him through the trees. His house all his life, that was his parents from their first married days, traces of the original foundation still visible in the yard. It was now a two-storey with a red door and windows, smoke rising from one of the two chimneys. A dark-green hedge surrounded the front of the house, at the side of which was a galvanised gate leading into the yard.

He stopped to let Hansie jump out to open the gate. She stood holding it back while Bernard drove through without even a nod. Keeper was sitting at the door and ran towards them, his tail wagging, but none of them acknowledged him as they made their way towards the house. The dog went to lick his hand but Bernard shoved him away and the dog cowered as if he had been beaten, slunk back towards the house where he lay down on the sacking against the wall.

Bernard took the box with the girls' mother in it from Carmel and put it on the mantelpiece between the chalk pheasants, the clock and a spike that speared all the receipts from the farm. Then he took off out the door, across the yard, through the gate, along the boreen to the high field.

The night was turning into its own bitterness again. Winter had come hurrying in one evening in November when he was locking up the gates and it still hadn't decided when it was going to leave. Right now he didn't care. Cold was what he was, inside and out.

He crossed into the next field, his head in turmoil, his mind burning. Synapses of rage ran through his body. He didn't know what was worse: that his wife had fucked another man or that she had died in a foreign country.

And now she was back.

Good old dependable Bernard, the stalwart. Always there, always there to pick up the pieces. But this was the final straw. How much was a man expected to take? Hadn't he done enough penance? Why this? Why another meal of misery that would bloat the bellies of the gossipers of the village for weeks?

Mrs Reid, Mrs Phelin, Mrs McGinley.

By the next morning they would wake up from a night of tossing and turning the story over and over in their heads to find that when they went to button their blouses and skirts they had fattened so much on his misfortune that their clothes wouldn't fasten. But that wouldn't stop them from still gorging at his and his girls' expense.

He came to the oak tree lying across his path, left as it was eighteen months since it was knocked down by the storms. He still hadn't got around to chopping it into firewood.

Remembering his wife was a match to the dry kindling of his heart and it was so close to igniting that he thought he would lose his breath. All of the time thinking she might come back. Deep down, even when he raged against what she had done to him, he willed her to return. All the time believing that he had left a part of himself with her that she never could renege on and it would draw her back to him with a twitch of a memory, a scent of new grass or a hand upon a sleeve.

But it never happened.

She left in darkness and came back the same way. When he heard the noise behind him he looked around.

It was Hansie.

'Daddy?'

'Go back into the house. Go back or the Pooka will get you', he shouted.

His daughter stopped.

'Go back now, I'm telling you, go back to the house right now and stop following me'.

He saw her shadow against the evening. Her outline in whatever light the frosty moon gave out made him even angrier. The way she inclined her young head. It was unbearable.

'Daddy?' The voice small and frightened.

'Go back home'.

Bernard gave a thin, weak laugh, watched the child's face crumble, her outstretched hand pulled back as if it had been smitten, then he watched her turn. The small frame scampered away, a frightened animal running for cover. A slight on the dark landscape.

A whisper of his wife fled from her as she ran.

He continued to walk, past the tree where he put hay in the crook of the branches for the black, white-headed cow. He crossed over walls, along paths that were made only by his feet, day after day, treading the same road.

There were few places where he didn't walk, with the way his land was parcelled out into lean pickings all over the place; few places he didn't know from all the times he went hunting with Keeper running beside him, loyal, willing to do anything for him, such fidelity, looking out for woodcock and grouse that rose spiralling from the undergrowth. He made it to the gap in the upper field and beyond the lake. The night was going to be a really cold one. He could tell by the sky. But what did it matter now?

He kept walking while the dark fell down behind the trees and night brought in more cold. It seeped through the fabric of his coat, his teeth were chattering as the damp came up through the earth. He sharpened his ears to the sound of the child returning, but all that came from behind the trees were strange squealings of animals fighting, worms burrowing, a fox keening.

That evening, two years before, when she hadn't come home, Bernard had warned the girls not to get out of bed, and went down the road to meet the last bus. He watched it come from far off, its lights disappear and return again as it went up and down the hills. It stopped at the gate entrance beyond him and the door opened, but only Pidgie Nowlan clunked down the steps with her four bags of shopping.

'Thanks, Eugene', she called back to the driver as the bus pulled away into the darkening and he heard the lonely sound of its going.

'What has you waiting?' she said, handing him two of the bags as if he had come especially to carry them for her.

'Sadie Naughton swore she'd have a clutch of day-olds down to me by today', he lied.

'Don't the dogs in the village know that she has more gluggers than the trees have leaves? Brigid Donoghue's a much safer bet, healthier chicks too. I thought that was Margaret's job, is she not the hen woman?'

She turned to him, her glasses slipping off her nose, as if she knew something. He didn't know why but he defended his wife saying something about one of the girls being sick and didn't want her mammy to leave her.

'Hansie is it? God knows but she's a delicate little thing, you'd need to mind her or she'll fall down on you all'. She took the bags from him and turned in her gate.

'They'll come tomorrow'.

'Who will?'

'The chicks you're waiting for', and without a *good night* or a *thank you* she shuffled up her own darkened path. He waited until she got in the door and saw the light come on in her kitchen. He made his way back to the house, tied the twine around the near gate, checked that the barn door was closed and locked in the hens. The girls were sitting up waiting for him, their faces tired, quizzical.

'Is mammy not with you?' Hansie had cried, stretching to look beyond him to check for her mother.

'No, she must be delayed. Maybe she went to Aunt Kate's and missed the bus?'

'She wouldn't have done that. She'd never do that without telling us, she wouldn't, she wouldn't', and she began to cry and kick the side of the dresser.

'None of that now or I won't let ye have toast before you go to sleep', he half-coaxed, half-chided. 'Come here let you, and help me rake up the coals. Aren't you the best girl at getting them good and red?'

He took the child's hand, put his own hand over it while they poked and raddled the fire until it began to glow again. He cut the loaf into slices and handed them a fork each.

They took it in turns holding the tines towards the front grill of the range then flipped the slices until there were brown bars gilding each side. Soon the kitchen was filled with the warm buttery scent.

He took Hansie up on one knee, Carmel on the other and held them there in the bowl of his lap until they had their supper eaten. When he ordered them off up to bed, Hansie started crying again, not wanting to go up without her mother. He picked her up; she snuggled into him as he walked up the stairs and put her in the bed beside her sister.

'Mind one another now', he said and went back down into the kitchen. Soon he could hear the hum of their prayers dripping through the floorboards, falling like blood onto the lino, the table cloth, in behind the cups and the saucers.

What was the animal that had come into the house? He felt it there long before it showed itself. He would come in after his day in the far field and he would smell it. A scent, the spoor of something he couldn't put a name on. Now he could.

He wished he could have deciphered it, to smoke it out of the house as if it had nested in the wallpaper feeding on the blousy peonies of the front room.

But it had evaded him until it was too late.

The afternoon before she left she had opened a little window of hope into a field with horse-chestnut trees when they could touch one another without hurting. A day stolen from summer. The plaid blanket she had folded up and brought with them spread out on the grass, the bottle of tea wrapped in it to keep it warm, Cidona and marble cake from the travelling shop for the girls. Her face was bright, open for the first time in months. Carmel and Hansie were playing, chasing up and down the fields, pulling the last of the daisies, threading them one into the other, a garland around their necks.

For a little while they forgot. They had talked about ordinary things like him clearing the boulders from the far field and how maybe they could think about getting in the water, building a bit of a bathroom, an indoor toilet. The girls came back to the blanket with an appetite on them and they munched into the egg scallion sandwiches and the marble cake. She started singing, *If I knew you were coming I'd have baked a cake,* and the girls picked up the chorus; the green all round them overwhelming them with its goodness, bringing with it a thimbleful of grace.

He remembered now how she had looked, the unusually warm air brightening her cheeks, the wind blowing a strand of her hair upwards, her skirt fanned out around her as she sat on the rug, a tiny dollop of hope spread thinly across the bread of their existence.

With that memory, he let out a roar like the cow did when the calf was stuck inside her, and it had to be cut out, its vernixed head lolling to the side, dead.

When Margaret went he gathered up whatever little pieces of his heart she had left to him that he might call his own. And up at the house was all that remained of her in a shining, lacquered, heartwood box with fine marquetry inserts sitting on the mantelpiece. What in all that was good and holy would he do with her ashes? The dust of what she had been burned to. Here was another kick in the teeth.

He stayed out in the field all night.

The sound of the sledgehammer echoed off the walls of the barn. Hansie was crying by now, quietly to herself, 'No, Daddy. No, Daddy', while Carmel stood with a face sour as bog. Again Bernard swung the hammer clean above his head and it came crashing down. He continued swinging and bringing down, the hardwood thinking it would get the better of him until it could no longer hold onto itself. The legs buckled, the oval leaves collapsed in a heap on top of one another, their sheen momentarily catching a shiver of light.

The table was now a sorry pile on the ground. Keeper broke his tether and came over near them, but not too near. Bernard stood, the muscles of the arm with the hammer attached, shaking uncontrollably. Then he dropped it. Its clang made them jump as he leaned his head back against the wall of the barn. All his strength had come to an end. Droplets of sweat fell from his forehead like tears, though they were not tears.

It began to rain, a bitter, sleety rain that soon soaked into his shirt. He could see it seep through the flannel of the girls' nightdresses. Drops splashed on the patina of the wood, and now little pearls of water soaked into its fragile skin and stained it, finally. Other drops sat like little worlds of their own on the pile of buckled legs, the oval leaves unrecognisable. It wasn't so much the pile of wood as the rain staining the surface that was too much for Hansie and she started to cry, loud and vicious like a fox in a trap. Bernard's teeth, firmly clenched up to this, opened just wide enough to say.

'What are you crying about? It's good riddance to bad rubbish. Come here to me'.

They shuffled close to him.

'Hold out your arms'.

They did his bidding and he filled them with the rubble of his exertion. They turned when Bernard ordered them to carry their bundles back into the room where the table once stood. Keeper slouched back in after them.

A stork's nest of twigs was already set in the grate of the parlour. Rolled up newspaper and dry kindling were waiting to be lit. Bernard struck a match and knelt down, pushed the light in under the paper. He stood back watching the smoke pour up through the twigs until it became flame and brightness. He took the smaller pieces of the hunting table and put them on first, waiting for each piece to catch before he put on the next. The girls sat on the sofa following the movement of Bernard's hand, reaching down to put another piece on the flames, the hardwood taking some time to ignite. Then it began to blaze and the heat came out to warm their faces.

Keeper crept close and lay on the rug in front of the fire surround, his head in his paws. Bernard could feel the flush of heat on his skin.

Margaret loved that table. It stood against the far wall of the parlour where the photo of her had hung, the one taken when she was a young girl and she had looked out at the world even then with the eye of one who longed to be somewhere else. She had a knack to the polishing of it, a knack that she had perfected, a mixture of linseed and wax that she blended and rubbed into the grain. Its surface was very delicate, absorbing the least stain and no one was allowed to place anything on it for fear they might spoil it. She looked after it as if she were preparing for some great event that only she was privy to.

It was kept covered with a cloth for most of the year and the only time it was really used was at Christmas. When he had all the jobs done in the yard he came in and after he washed his hands she took the bottle of sherry from the hunting table and poured him a little glass – just to show there was no ill feeling – whatever she meant by that.

He bought it for her just because she asked. He had sold some cattle and put the money aside. He searched house after old house for it, had worked his way among chalked lots in basements and old barns before he finally found it when the Osfelts sold up. She spun stories to the children about how it would stand proud in the courtyard, set out with salmon, pork pies, meat of every kind, the stamping of horses and braying of hounds all around. The spicy scent of hot ports.

What did it ever do but bring them misery?

'A good fire', his mother used to say, when misfortune heaped itself upon a family, 'a good fire was the only thing to clear it out'.

He watched as the blaze was reflected in the glass cabinet on the far wall. Tongues of flame licked up the curves of the cups, the jugs, and gobbled them. So surrounded were they by the flames and their mirroring in the glass that for a moment it looked like they were sitting in the centre of a small hell. As the heat spread out, the cold within him loosened its grip and his shirt began to steam. The smell of his own body rose up from his skin, a familiar, homey smell that made him aware of himself again and mingled with the smells of the girls, the dog.

When the last leg of the table caught fire, he sat back in the chair beside his daughters and something fell from his body then, a shadow maybe that slipped onto the floor, into the fire and was consumed by the wood's flame. His shoulders straightened as if he were someone else while his wife's ashes stood above it all on the mantelpiece.

This Street with Looking-Glass Eyes

'Bring me back great stories', Andrew's sister says. She is sitting up in bed, her arms clasped around her knees, blue eyes waiting for him to sweep them clean of any dreams. 'Bring me back a big slice of the city in your rucksack'.

'With or without pepperoni', he jokes. Then he leans over, kisses her cheek and picks up his keys. He files away the tall order she has presented him with and heads out the door, pulling his parka more tightly around him as he hits the cutting air.

He makes his way along the street towards the shops. People are already moving in and out of the day. He walks by the square where the homeless are scavenging the bins of the homed. They pull out chicken bones, empty pockets of pitta bread; upend a can of cola to see if it still has a dreg of sugar left inside.

He burrows his way through the aisles of the supermarket; buys what's needed to keep flesh under their skin and heads back to where she is waiting for him.

How thin his sister, how very sad her eyes.

'What have you brought me?' she enquires.

'A bowl of fresh morning air'.

He curves his hands and holds them to her face. When she feels the cold of the new day on his fingers, she caresses them before she secrets her own hands back under the duvet.

He sets up a tray for her, ricotta from the new cheesemongers, bread still smelling of the oven it was saved from, some wild acacia honey. He takes out a fresh napkin depicting a scene of girls and bridges and blue weeping willow, tucks it under her chin.

'My very own restaurant', she says, as she plays with dripping bee sweetness onto the bread, moves it around the plate he has placed before her. Stocks and shares fall on the other side of the city. Mortgages default. Businesses fold in on themselves while she cuts the bread into little cubes; stacks them into columns three squares high, playing with them like a child; pretends she doesn't see his frown, his threats if she doesn't eat. She knows that she is pushing her luck with him. Finally, she takes a mouse-bite out of the wheaten loaf.

'Where are my stories?' she demands, lifting the napkin to brush crumbs from her mouth. So, he tells her, embellishes the things he has seen on his shopping expedition. How there were archaeologists excavating ruins near the top of the square. A woman in a high-vis jacket was sweeping soil from the bones of an ancient bird with a small paintbrush while a man numbered shards of plates that still held a tracery of leaves and vines. Another unearthed a collection of battered drinking vessels with the memory of some magic potion. Some day it would teach the world to sing.

Her eyes open wide, imagining the world of outside where things happen. 'All those things you can see in a single trip', she says.

'It's simple', he replies. 'All you have to do is look'.

She pours milk on top of the black underworld of Java and sips her coffee, spoon after spoon. How thin she is, how very pale her skin.

Today he places a bowl of peas in front of her and she doesn't baulk at the task of splitting pods to reveal each pea that clings to the other. Silently she separates them. This is progress, he says to himself and he is grateful. In the early days she wouldn't even let him open the curtains. They had to practise the art of pulling the linen fabric inch by knife-blade inch every day, opening to a scimitar of light until they finally got to the stage where a whole shaft of it spread across the beechwood floor. Now she sits by the open window, the lace of the curtain blowing softly in the breeze; the light coming from the left as she bends over the bowl of legumes, counting each perfect green sphere. In another life she would have been captured by the brush of Metzu. Oil on Panel. 'A Young Woman Shelling Peas', the model's fragility underscored by the delicate blossom in the foreground.

This work soon tires her and she goes to lie down. It is her way of letting go of the world. Little snatches every day and night when she falls into sleep and blocks out the birds, the sky and the purse of mist above the park.

When they were left with no one but themselves, their mother's sister, Aunt Vera, came and took them to her house beyond the city. She did what no other could do for them. She held them in the calm of her compassion while his sister screamed and sobbed her life out into the sleeve of her blue cardigan. People kept calling to the door, talking in whispers, wondering if they could help. There was a newly-baked round of soda bread cooling on the windowsill. When no one was looking his sister took a chunk out of it and put it in her pocket. Now that she was lost she needed the crumbs to find her way back home. Aunt Vera never let on but blamed the magpies in the big ash tree at the top of the field with branches that spread out like a pair of human lungs. Every day Andrew looked out at that tree when he thought his breath wouldn't come. He followed its example: in, out, in, out, the oxygen flowing into bronchioles, alveoli, the language of airwaves he learned about in biology class.

They stayed with their aunt until he got his first job with an accountancy firm. He bought, just before the boom, a place of their own, with his half of their parents' legacy. It was one of the houses that no one wanted, on the wrong side of the river, all dark and dank, but he got light into it where there was light to come in, French doors leading out to the small yard, a garden in pots, sun chairs. The other half of the house was used to set up a dance studio for his sister. People marvelled at their good luck. A sure sign that their parents were looking after them, getting it at a fraction of the price, walls of mirrors, a practice bar, classes filling up, news spreading, ballet, tap shoes tapping.

How well she had been managing, until now.

The sights and sounds of Monday mornings carry nothing new. The list goes like this: commuters sitting in their cars listening to the doom of the early news; shutters of shops being pulled open; feet everywhere on the footpath rushing towards the people they love or darting away from those they don't. A child drags his school bag all along the pavement on his way to class. Andrew spends the day revising his images so when he gets home he tells his sister about the boy walking his green iguana on a yellow lead through the gates of the school. He paints the sagging dewlap under the lizard's throat, the crest of scales curling down its back, the brown bands along its green tail. He describes its predicament: how it was only able to work the circumference of its lead that was tethered to the boy's left ankle. When it tried to stray further than its own space the small boy stamped on the piece of rope. The creature lashed out with its tail, the black orb of its eye staring at the world.

'Charlita', he says, 'the iguana was called Charlita'.

It is almost three years since that day when his sister arrived home with her eyes closed, willing herself to be blind. Something that day, something she saw when she was walking by the river as the waters churned up and rolled towards the sea, something that day did it. A lone swan, too white for the oil gathering on its feathers, swam by and there near the bridge a shopping trolley careened on the bank, half-in, half-out of the water, drowning, river-slime clinging to its bars. She came in and sat in the corner of the room, the wildness of a forest in her eyes. Andrew spent the evening soothing her until she was able to speak clearly. And what she said was this.

'I have walked home with ghosts each side of me, and I will never do that again. Parents don't have to leave you at the edge of the woods without breadcrumbs just to forsake you. How can I ever find my way back home again?'

'You are home now', he reassured her as he held her in his arms.

Another day's work is upon him. He goes to the office downtown, glad to be out, glad that there is a job to go to. Sharp enough to skin and fillet a fish all in one go, the wind coming up the river slaps him in the face as he searches out everything that might have a story hidden in it. Something he can bring back home in the evening.

He meets up with Janice at lunchtime. They go to the new café that sells anti-recession food, big farmer's helpings that keep a whole den of wolves from the door.

She knows about his sister, how she lives in the dark room of their house and will not go out. She looks at him over the menu.

'You're doing her no favours', she says as she bites into the lamb shank and tears flesh from the bone. 'She is sucking the life from you, can't you see it? Sinking her teeth into your neck. She will drain the marrow from your soul'.

'That's not the way it is at all', he snaps.

'What age is she now, thirty ... thirty-five?'

'Thirty three'.

'If she was Jesus she'd be crucified. Instead she's crucifying you'.

'You don't understand'.

Janice just shakes her head and mutters something about leeches.

All afternoon he thinks of what his friend has said as he tries to balance the black flies of numbers that crawl in columns all over the Excel sheet he is hoping to make some sense of. He loves his sister. When she cries, he tastes salt.

The inquest confirmed it was an accident. The brakes failed, nothing more, crashed into the barrier at the docks, into the roiling water with no going back. Their parents gone in an instant that day and his sister poised to enter her first major competition the other side of the country. Aunt Vera taking her there and driving her back before she sat down to break them with the news, clenching in her broad, rough hands his sister's winning certificate.

He waits for his computer to shut down, heads for home. Dinner to buy, new stories to forage for along the dingy pavements. And Janice's words stinging nettle deep.

He walks, drinking up the well of the street, the sounds of cars and the escaping smells from the sewers; draws in the colour of the falling night. He passes a group of young boys on the far side of the square, outside an old red brick house, with a big FOR SALE sign tied to the railings. They are pulling a smashed mirror as big as a door from the skip on the pavement outside it. Its dark frame, carved in acanthus leaves and pomegranates, towers over them. Remaining slivers of looking glass tinkle to the ground and two of them busy themselves gathering up the jagged edges from the pavement. The street light glints off the mirror shards and tiny unseen worlds are reflected back. Two of the others are straightening up the frame, their jaws set with determination. Their wiry bodies scaffold each side of it while the fifth boy on the skateboard gets himself ready some distance back from them.

Andrew stands and watches. With his knees bent, the skater pushes hard off his back foot; then he brings his front knee forward and pops the nose of the board into the air. He clears through the frame, slides his foot towards the nose of the board and lands the jump confidently at the other side of the broken mirror. The cheers of his friends fill the night air. As he does a semi-circular lap of honour around Andrew the young boy catches his eye: 'Would you like to have a look at yourself, Mister', he says, 'a real good look at yourself?'

By the time he gets home winter has fallen on their side of the street. His sister is sitting by the lamp, reading. She looks up from her page. The light from the bulb shines on the open book. Half her face is in shadow, he can only see one of her eyes.

'What great stories have you brought me this time?' she says and smiles. Behind that bright eye is a life refusing to be lived. Andrew searches around for any words that might spell themselves out for her. He leaves down his bag, starts to unbutton his coat.

'None', he says to her. 'This evening our street is all out of stories'.

Frost Heave

Night and the bitterness so much in his mouth that Folan could taste his own liver. The moon full, full over the stone walls, the fields, silvering all it shone on; air frost killing the hedge around him as he sat crouched in the back of the henhouse. He held his shotgun close, the cold biting into his hands so that he had to squeeze them under his oxters to keep the feeling alive in them. That morning he had come out, cats scratching at the door for their breakfast, and found six of his hens scattered across the dirt-floor of their coop, heads lolling to one side, the blood sucked out of them. Killing for sport, killing just to taste death.

He blew on his hands again, his breath chilled before it ever got to them. He was tired of things being taken from him. He hadn't seen it coming. He hadn't seen it at all.

He had filled himself with the dinner before he came out. At times like this it helped to have a full belly, though he was beginning to get tired of the meat that stuffed his freezer. Still, too good to be wasted. A couple of weeks earlier, out hunting, he had come across the stag lying in the ditch. Beautiful beast. Struck by a carload of lads coming back from the pub; left lying there. Folan had taken the gun from his shoulder, pulled off his jacket and covered its indigo marble eye, glassy with pain. The import of the shot rang through the woods and was muffled by the trees as the upper body shuddered. The hind quarters, already broken, never moved.

It was a bitch to get the animal into the trailer but he did and drove it back, pulled it into the yard with its powerful antlers all rutted out. He winched it up into the roof of the barn with a pulley. Bled it, grallocked it. The ease with which the pelt came away, the animal still warm, like it had just slipped off its coat in an overheated room.

Ireland falling into the ice age and the carcass froze right through to the ribs. No choice the next morning but to take the chainsaw to it and carve it up as best he could, the meat all jag-damaged at the edges as he piled it already frozen into the freezer. It would take him a lifetime to eat so much flesh on his own.

Now.

Too many sounds to take care of in one go. Cars over the road, Tim McCann's dog beyond the fields howling, some night bird shrilling 'here, here', bewildering his thoughts. The last four hens clucked and settled into their roosts. How to sharpen his hearing enough to pick up the stealth of animal coming towards him, searching out its sport? He pulled his jacket around him, dragged red out of his cigarette. The glow of it. He had buried the wire two foot down into the ground and the cunt of an animal had found a weakness along its length, mayhem and feathers everywhere. He could wait it out; he would wait it out until blood began to congeal in his veins with the cold.

If that's what it took.

The way realisation suddenly crept up on him and kicked him in the teeth. That day, one of the horses had torn its fetlock on a piece of rusted metal. The only cure sea water and he trying to coax the animal into the trailer without any more damage done to it. He had to ask Gretta to come out and help him. She agreed, even decided to go as far as the beach with him. He thought that was something, couldn't remember when they last did that together. But there she was, sitting up high beside him, pushing the day along with her chatter, eating up the miles with gossip about Bill Taylor's wife and how she had cleaned out their bank account after buying a greenhouse to start sowing her own vegetables. Bill only discovered it when the oil man came to fill the tank and he went to take out cash to pay him.

Folan felt good that day on the way to the beach, the sound of the horse clomping in the back, the air-freshener swinging its scent of pine back and forth from the rear-view mirror, Saint Christopher holding onto the sacred child for dear life. Every now and then he looked across at his wife as she chatted away, the grey roots showing down the centre of her skull, a tiny turkey wattle forming under her chin. She was going on and on about how they had lived more years together than they had as single people. He thought she was saying that this was a good thing.

The tide coming in. Folan walked the horse up and down in the waves, whispering to it, the salt clearing poison from the wound. He looked back to see Gretta as she strolled the strand, picking up bits of flotsam, her wax jacket flapping in the breeze. And something about her startled him. Something about her that he didn't recognise. As if a creature had come in from the sea and enveloped her so that the wife he looked at was the wife he couldn't see. A great loneliness came down over him then. He wanted to run to her and put his hands on her face and feel the warmth of her while he promised her a new microwave, a maple tree, the heavens.

The start of the end of things. He walked the horse up the beach to where she now sat etching hieroglyphics into the sand with a piece of stick. He held the reins of the horse tightly to him.

'You're making great shapes there', he said to her.

'Did you know', she replied, 'that the word UNITED becomes UNTIED with the change of an "I"?'

What could he say to that?

Caged once, the animal. Like all the others round it. Circling and circling in its miniscule wire prison, its tinny squeak as it pushed its nose to the wire in an attempt to get out. Finding the cage door open, tumbling out into the wild, webbed feet on the ground as the air sleeked its guard hairs, its dense under-fur keeping heat in. Thriving in its solitary state. Tracks on the snow, tracks on the frosted grass.

Scats.

What a gobdaw he was not to have taken much notice at first – of Gretta uploading photos onto her Facebook page. When she complained that they never did anything together any more, he joined up himself just to show he was not going against her, to prove her wrong. But it bored him and the more it bored him the more she was fired up about it. She said she liked to look at other people's lives. Strangers' stories sent a picture to her brain of her own blood pushing its way through veins and arteries into the tiniest of capillaries until she felt there were strings of lights switching on through the pathways of her body. It made her feel she was still alive. That is what she said to him when he complained about her jumping up and running across to the little table under the window to see if the latest person who had 'friended' her had posted their photos of a trip to Prague or Barcelona. She had never been to either place. Folan was not one for travelling. He loved the land around him – his father's, his grandfather's before that. He believed that if everyone stayed in their own spot the world would be better off.

They argued.

'There's a whole world out there to be conquered', she said, crumbs of toast blackening her teeth. She had 'friended' Hull and Lorient and Wellington: old friends that she hadn't heard from since she had been a teller in the bank or struggling at Weight-Watchers. She posted photos of herself standing with the horses at the Horse Fair, while all around her men were spitting on palms as tight rolls of money changed hands. She was pleased with how she looked. He told her the light flattered her.

He shivered. Should have read the signs, should have noticed the way she started learning a new language. Going around practising like she was in the thick of plans for her first foreign holiday. Cutlery became silverware. She served him ground beef instead of good old reliable mince that she had been buying from Rooney's butchers since they were first married. She didn't go to the pictures with Bill Taylor's wife any more. No, it was the movies, now.

'You're watching too many of them American shows', Folan told her.

'Which ones?' she said.

He waited it out until she had gone to her step-aerobic classes. She was determined to keep trim, not letting mid-life flibflab its way across her middle. A few days before when he had brought over a trailer-load of manure for her rosebeds, Bill Taylor's wife had said something about Gretta's privacy settings. Though he was shaken, he didn't let on. The whole world now knew her business. He pulled up her Facebook page. He could see the comments written, the photos on her wall. He saw her status. *Single.* 'Did she think a shotgun was too intimate?' some Tom was asking her. Something about a black powder rifle, a Shiloh Sharps, though modern-made as near he could get to the real thing. This guy was going on and on about the excitement of getting as close to his game as possible, knowing that there was only one shot to get your kill, one shot, that's all. But Tom would teach her. He would make sure she learned that.

Was he fucking serious? She couldn't handle a wooden spoon without dropping it.

A whole list of replies:

Way to go, Gretta.

Mighty stuff.

Wish it was me, Gretta.

Folan had been out treating some of his sheep who were infected with orf. When he got back, she was sitting at the table, a glass empty but for ice melting over a slice of lemon beside her. She was studying the ingredients from the gin bottle. He slipped off his wellingtons in the scullery and reached for his boots. There was a pot of potatoes for the hens bubbling on the range. She started to read out the list of herbs that were etched into the glass on each side of the gin bottle: juniper berries and orris root, grains of paradise.

'Why?' He asked her. 'To be thinking of going when things are not that bad; when things are not bad enough to go'.

'Not bad enough is no longer good enough. We might as well have a red triangle at the end of our bed, like a broken car pulled in on the hard shoulder, to warn anything coming behind us that we have broken down'.

She laughed at that.

She couldn't even be serious about things that were serious.

'Some little seed of fun, of paradise', she looked up at him. 'That's all. I don't want to wake up some wet morning to discover that there is nothing but a long string of misery to pull us through the next part of our life. And this, certainly not this', she said, waving her hand over the kitchen with steam rising up and condensing on the one window that let in a bit of light.

'Do you have to?'

'Look', she said, pointing to where his chair was beside the fire. The lino tiles were worn into the ground where he placed his feet every evening. 'You'll bore yourself into the middle of the earth from staying in the one spot for too long. That's not going to be me. I'm dying here'.

UNITED became UNTIED in the blink of an 'I'. An American taking the eye of his wife while the mink played puck with his Orpingtons.

He lost respect for himself for a while afterwards. He slept all day, wide awake all night, walking across his fields when he could barely see where he was going, the moon shut behind the clouds. His trousers hung on him like a scarecrow, *a fear bréige*, a false man. He took a mat from the back door and covered the hole he had drilled into the lino. That only made it worse.

These things he missed about her as he listened for the animal across the frost: her heading off to town to get the two-for-one offers on yoghurts or marmalade; ham with its use-by-date well past. How she laughed, throwing her head back, showing enough mercury to drive a hatter mad. The way he liked to watch her bend over when she was taking the clothes from the washing machine, her breasts hanging down, in them black leggings, all rump and broad haunch.

A favourite cow.

The day she left she told him she was tired of eternally wondering what was going to meet her around corners. She wanted to be able to drive down a straight line of road, watch a car rise dust in the distance and wave to it as it passed her by, going in the opposite direction.

He followed all her actions on Facebook. The whole world knew about her whitewater rafting and the cycling, as well as driving her truck into great hills of snow. She was smiling out at him, holding up a snow rake that had precipitated a roof avalanche on top of her. Covered in white and laughing. He could imagine the snow that found its way down behind her scarf, melting as it touched the heat of her neck. She was pontificating about frost heaves as if she had never heard of potholes. She hadn't realised, until she was where other people were, that this was where she wanted to be, she told anyone and everyone that bothered to read what she wrote.

Sounds wonderful, Gretta.

Wish I could be you, Gretta.

That's some man you've got there, Girl.

He could see her in the General Store, with its good old-fashioned charm. She was one of '*the communidy*' now. The *t* softened to *d*, letting go of her own tongue to suck on someone else's. Boars-head meat beside favourite frozen novelties. Walking in, being greeted by Barbara behind the counter. How rage boiled up in him. Lee Saoul playing her guitar over the soft rustle of newspapers as people turned them over and filled their coffee cups again, called out to her. A pan in the kitchen being scraped and potatoes mashed while she bought pastrami on rye, linguica, corned beef hash for her Tom.

At least he wasn't called Bud. Bud would have killed him entirely. That name opening up to her petal by petal. Sitting in the front yard on a love seat, a fucking loveseat with his square jaw and his hair streaked back, a cold beer, full-fitting jeans; blue jays in the trees.

She posted up pictures of their sugar house. Night temperatures cold enough to send the sap rushing back down the bole of the tree, followed by a warm day that drew it right up again. The two of them in their big, red ass pick-up as they drove out to the sugar bush, striking it while the sap was running, boring into the trees, the spigot drip, drip into the pail, bucket, whatever she called it now. All day and night the stove fed with kindling as they boiled off the water, reducing it all to sweetness. Bleeding sweetness out of the sugar bush as if she were born to it. Drinking in all its sickening sap.

Could she not have waited for his sugar time, good old promises between her lips, instead of packing up and taking the bus to the airport, fuck-friend waiting for her at the other end with his Shiloh Sharps.

She told him when they were first married that she liked the way they lay in bed, his hand above her breasts, his thumb and fingers splayed out each side of her neck, her throat, lying there as they slept. Sometimes he would lift his index finger and stroke her jaw-line before they fell asleep, dreaming their own dreams. She said that she never worried about him having his fingers so close to her throat in the way a lion tamer doesn't fear the animal in front of him. She trusted him. She liked to think that even though he could do it, could so easily squeeze the life out of her, that he wouldn't; that he never would. Never. He could barely flatten a midge that took lumps out of his face when they were in the bog cutting turf. She loved that sense of danger. Sleeping with a man who had such power and didn't realise it; never let it go to his head. She loved that in a man.

It wasn't enough though, was it?

In the end.

He lit another cigarette. The moon continued to shine down on him, on the henhouse, on the rustle of animal musking up the place as it made its way close, the ground so hard, earlier that day they had to take a jackhammer to poor old Patch Murray's grave to break up the soil. Two feet down they had to go before they hit earth soft enough to bury him. As they stood breastfeeding their shovels, the gravediggers laughed that it was the frigid wife below Patch that had the ground frozen. They knew for a fact, other parts of the graveyard would not be so cold. 'A warm wife is what you need. A warm wife with staying power'. Tights Reilly sneered out of the side of his mouth as he took a swig from the bottle of whiskey.

Bigger than a stoat, smaller than an otter. Brought across the Atlantic for its fur, lustrous sheen so thick it didn't need to hibernate. Could be out in this weather, any weather, the lake frozen and no fish, its sharp eyesight picking out the henhouse. Jaws primed to close on the last of his chickens. Its winter pelt so luxurious he would have made a stole for her out of it. To keep her neck cosy, warm, while she was raking snow from the roof. Now, she could have put that up on Facebook.

Drinking His Strength Back

I come upon him first in the fruit and veg aisle. What with the tangled hair, streeling behind him, the crusty beard, leather sandals with the thong thingies criss-crossed on his shins, a blanket thrown across his shoulder he looks for all the world like he was dredged up from the Flat Lake Festival. He's chomping on a carrot as if he has one serious attack of the munchies, the green ferny tops sticking out of the side of his mouth.

I turn the corner and there he is again slouched against a column in the tinned food section. People are sparring their way around him with their trolleys, children pulling at cans of spaghetti hoops, moshing them down on top of soft-sliced pans that aren't even fit for swan consumption. He's standing there with a John West tin of salmon in his hand; you know the wild red one all the way from ball-freezing Alaska, and he's pressing his thumb against the label.

Then he puts it to his mouth, the thumb that is, sucks it. Somewhere above the clatter and squeak of trolleys, a disembodied voice is telling the lot of us all that there's a special offer on sunscreen. Ha! Fat chance of needing that.

As sure as eggs is eggs, don't I see Crusty again as I make my way towards the till. This time he's pulling a packet of condoms off the shelf. Mr Supersonic Turbo-charged Security man is eyeing him up ready to pounce. Thankfully, Crusty returns the highly sensitive all-your-Christmases-come-at-once pack to where he got it and then starts on the AAA batteries. Trolleys hit off his shins, a child is having a blue tantrum blowout and Crusty cowers below the onslaught. The Mother Theresa in me surfaces and I reach out and tug his jacket. 'Are you ok?'

'Am I in hell or what?' he whispers.

'I wouldn't say tonight's that bad. You should come on a Friday night when …'

But he's not listening.

'I have to get out of here; back to my men … must see if they survived, if they're still alive'.

I'm not sure what grow house he's just come from but up close I notice the scratches on his face, his arms in flitters, his hands all blood. He's been in the wars all right. Some gangland fiasco, no doubt, and I pull myself away. But Mother Theresa whispers in my ear again and I find I'm at the checkout, paying for his tins of salmon and putting them in my bag with my quarter pound of mince, my dinners for one.

When we get out into the fresh air he's like a dog with his first porcupine, he just doesn't know what to do. Wherever his mind is, it's not in the car park as he manoeuvres himself gingerly in and out through the bonnets and boots, touching them, then jumping back. The Luas is another story altogether.

'Serpent', he growls, pulls out a sword from beneath his blanky and swashbuckles towards the monster-iron snake. But it gets away just in time. What can I do but distract him with a bar or two of *More than a Woman* and when I finally settle him we walk across the bridge, me still singing. Mothers pushing buggies stare at us; teenagers carrying their bicycles down the steps take no notice. The sun's beginning to give up on the day.

'I'm Tara, by the way'.

'Finn', he says.

'Oh, cool'.

'No! Mac. MacCumhaill'.

Surely, he can't be serious.

Mary Stephens is out weeding her little patch as we turn into the estate. She's as good as Sky News and I know that before I have the code punched into the alarm, my life will have gone viral. Lucky greets us at the door, his black and white head bobbing in delight, his tail wagging. I take my cue from this little dog. He's my man barometer. When Finn kneels down to rub him, the dog starts licking his hand straight away.

'Lucky's giving you the ok', I say happily. 'Good dog'.

I relax.

It takes all of five minutes for my not-so-smart-phone to ring. It's Mags.

'Please, don't tell me that's the dodgy guy from the speed-dating night in there with you?'

'No, it's not. He's just a bit lost that's …'

'Aren't we all? But that's not enough reason to bring home an indigent'.

'A wha ...'

'You get my drift. You must be out of your tree. Did the last fiasco not teach you any thing? You'll end up on the front page of all the Red Tops, Garda tape wrapped around the house like it's a Christmas tree, TV cameras poking through the windows; the lot'.

'You're being a tad melodramatic, Mags'.

'Well, don't come whinging to me if you're found dismembered at the end of the garden'.

She clicks off in a huff.

'With friends like that', I say to Finn, pointing at my mobile.

'Why are you talking to a funny bone?' he wonders.

I laugh, funny bone, that's a good one. Hmm ...

I bring him into the sittingroom.

He looks around and shivers. 'I will light your fire', he says, staring into my eyes. His are ceanothus blue. Oh, crap. Mags was right, my pesky dog wrong. What to do? Scream?

But no. Finn's looking at my lifeless grate, stuffed with junk mail, Magnum wrappers, cigarette butts and before you can say *Desperate Housewives,* he's taking two pieces of flint from his boot, striking them together and has flames roaring up the chimney in no time.

'Like home', he says.

I leave him in the capable paws of Lucky and head out into the kitchen.

When I come back with the dinner, don't I find him fast asleep on the floor, the sheepskin rug that me and Jimmy fought over in the divorce, wrapped around him. I'm a sucker for men when they're asleep; the little drool out the side of their mouths, the slight frown, their sweet breathing; they look so ... so manageable. I give a little cough, touch his shoulder and he sits up with a start, goes immediately to his sword.

'Don't worry', I say quietly, 'there's no battle here'.

I cross-leg on the floor beside him and hand him a plate. He struggles with the *spag bol,* slurping it from his hands into his mouth.

'Nice worms'.

Jimmy Waldron never said anything as complimentary about my food. Ever.

So there we are, on the floor, our backs to the couch, sipping the Red Breast that's left over from the divorce party. The heat warms my face, the scent of mountain and stream easing from his clothes and my tongue gets itchy.

'So what happened?'

He licks his plate till it's like it's had a double wash in Sun tablets.

'We were out hunting ...'

'Where?'

'Way beyond the upper Dodder valley. We were in pursuit of a particularly fine stag, Bran and Sceolan barking and chasing the prize. The day was so fine I didn't know which gladdened my heart more, the birds singing in the glen or the fine antlers of the stag as we gained on it'.

A poet and he doesn't know it. This man'd be some catch if he was catchable.

'Their triumphant cry', he continues, 'echoed through the hills as they brought it down. We were heading towards my own mountain, Seefin, when we came upon three beautiful women who offered us food and drink'.

'As women do', I say, swirling the last of my whiskey in the glass.

'The sun was at its hottest and we were glad to sit and drink with them, our prize catch ready to bring home, the dogs sleeping off the chase. I could hear the men laughing and courting the women as I went off to cut out the heart of the stag for the dogs. And then it happened'.

'What did?'

'They all went silent one by one. I crept back to where they were and what I saw chilled my blood. My men were frozen like statues among the gorse and the heather. I threw the stag's heart at the women and they drew swords on me, screaming as the blood spattered all over them'.

His voice went all funny as he said. 'Then before my eyes all their beauty began to fall away. Their hair turned grey, skin wrinkled, teeth rotted in their mouths'.

'I know the feeling, exactly', I say. 'Full body meltdown'.

But he doesn't seem to hear me. He's gone somewhere else.

'The most awful sound then came from their shrivelled mouths that was straight out of hell. Such high-pitched screams told me that if I didn't get out of there I was in the most terrible of dangers'.

He's right there. Bad enough one deranged woman, let alone three. But I zip it while he tells me that as they were cleaning the blood out of their eyes, he crawled through the furze and snaked along the ground. He could hear them still screaming while he headed towards an underground chamber which had an exit to the other side of the mountain. But when he came out where he thought he was coming out his whole landscape had changed.

'Some devilish beast must have come and eaten up the passageways because I couldn't find my normal route. Then I end up in that terrifying place. What did you call it?'

'The Square? You think that's bad? Property developers! You should see what they did to the rest of the country. Made a dog's dinner of it. And now they've all gone up the swanny without a helipad'.

'The dog's dinner. Where?'

'Never mind'.

'I need to get back to my men, see what's happened to them'.

'As soon as it's dark, I'll drive you'.

'In your chariot?'

'No, my Ka. It may not be to your standard but to me but it's still a legend'.

We throw on more logs and we sit there talking. I'm itching to switch on *Sex in the City* but I can't take a chance after what he's been through with the mad women. One look at it and my flatscreen will be flattened. Where will I be then?

When I see Mary Stephens across the street pulling her curtains on the evening I know it's time to move. I have a bit of a job coaxing him into the passenger seat because his sword keeps catching in the bobbly seat covers. Not a sinner takes any notice of us as I drive towards the shops, out onto the Old Bawn Road, down by the Mill House and round the roundabout. Finn is hanging onto the dashboard as I rumble up towards Bohernabreena. 'I got my licence first time', I tell him but he doesn't seem to be impressed by that little nugget of information. We drive up the snaking roads, take the turn for Glenasmole. Only when he starts to recognise his hunting ground does he relax. As Seefin comes into view I stop the car and he jumps out.

'You're a good woman', he says as he touches my cheek. Pity Jimmy Waldron didn't think so.

Then he's gone.

I watch him walk into the heather as the mountain comes towards him, see a change come over him as if he drinks his strength back into himself. His stature increases, he stands tall and brave. Then I hear his call echo across the mountains; his warrior shadow gets darker and darker as he climbs towards the sky. I reverse my little blue chariot and head towards home. As I drive back down the mountain I watch the lights of the city eating up the dark; notice how easily they block out the stars.

THE DEVIL'S DYE

First Eliza must chase Marisolle from the barn. That girl with her pangolin eyes and slouching walk carries bad spirits in her pocket and every time she is within bleeding distance things start to unhappen. She is best sent off to the fields at the end of the farm where she can sit in the blistering heat and hex no one, float around the corn shucks; let the *duende* of her mind dance like a mad thing – if that's what a goblin does – but not here. Not here in the barn where Eliza knows everything depends on it, the plantation's livelihood, their house, their mother's nervous disposition.

Eliza gathers as many bundles of the plant into her arms as she can manage and piles them into the expanse of vat that squats on the dusty floor. She orders the servants to carry buckets of water from the cistern to the big zinc bath, pour. The colour a dirty yellow, the odour so offensive it chokes the whole space around them and they have to pull their aprons over their mouths, their noses, as they continue to bring more buckets to its rim.

'Go now. Leave me', she says. 'Go about your other chores and leave me, for this is my task only'.

She waits until Nathanial and Amos pull the big door closed and apart from the light that comes through the slats of the windows and the motes that scatter out around her, there is just herself and the putrid container of mud liquid before her.

It started with an envelope from Antigua. She had taken the letter knife and slipped it under the paper. Out spilled a handful of seeds. Another of her father's follies, something he believed while he was away, something that would keep the house from the bankers. Before that it was alfalfa, and before that again, ginger. Rice had, of course, been the preferred crop up to this, but the War of Jenkins' Ear had put paid to that. He had a notion that the land on the plantation could grow anything, anything that was capable of being put in the ground.

But he was proven wrong time and time again.

Then the yellow seeds came. They filled her with courage as she held them in her hand. She thought of him away from his family, trying to keep everything going. He reminded her that she was in the battlefield, just like he was. Every morning she had to dress as if she was facing a new confrontation and she had to force her spirit into the place where it would not be overcome, no matter what. A human heart was more than that. A human heart could take a lot more.

She planted the yellow seeds. She watched them grow.

Thunder sky, charred egrets' bones, midnight clouds. Bruise. She knows that within the swirling vat of brown sludge and stench in front of her it is there. Somewhere. She knows that, as forcefully as she knows that blood follows cut. But how to get it to reveal itself to her, to pull it out, to let it transform itself in front of her, the colour that Newton found, hidden in there between the blue and the violet? So elusive, as if it wasn't there at all, and only by the magic of air would it appear.

She stirs the vat again.

When the voices of the servants disappear into the trees, she slips off her clothes until she is down to her white lace petticoat and bloomers. She picks up the paddle that Amos has fashioned for her and steps into the vat. Soon she is up to her knees in the muddy water. She takes the oar and starts to slap the liquid with it. She keeps on beating until she has whipped up a foam, bubbles rising and frothing in front, behind and all around her.

She beats out the frustration inside her; all those disappointments over the years, all those failed harvests. Plants pushing through the earth, the hope of that. Then frost-ruin, the leaves wilted and turned to mush, God punishing her, pulling the sky further and further up into the firmament.

She thrashes out that year when the seeds broke through the ground, put their shoots down into the earth and stretched up to the light. Until the caterpillars came. They came from the cocoons that had sheltered in the eaves of the house, hatched out of their husk eggs and crawled over the leaves, clearing them as if they were a fire. What was left of the plants was burnt by the sun.

She beats the liquid because her father is away at war and can't look after the house. It is left to her. Only. She wallops the back of the water as if it is a slave who has stolen a pig from the pantry. She beats it and beats it until the perspiration drips from her forehead into her eyes and everything becomes a haze.

She waits.

Until.

The surface becomes covered with foam, bubbles of navy surrounding her. Blue bleeds itself towards the violet, and violet steals back from itself. She jumps out of the vat, lets the water drip from her and as the linen of the petticoat meets with the air it begins to happen. Her once white underclothes change like alchemy from the dirty brown to the colour of midnight, magpie feather, soot, shadow-mountain: Indigo.

The Best Man for the Job

Dolores was lambasting me, as usual, for *thoosin'* around the window like a bluebottle and the night pitch black, but I could hear bouncing out in the garden.

'It's just your tinnitus acting up, again', she said so I rubbed my breath off the window and peered out. Yep, there it was, a silvery light bouncing; someone out there kangarooing up and down on my grand-daughter's trampoline. So I told her straight out.

'Well, go and prove me wrong so, if you're that sure'.

I hate when she says that. I know she'll eat me without salt if she's right.

'But I'm in my pyjamas'.

'For God's sake, Jimmy, I'm not asking you to parade around Grafton Street in your pelt. You're in your own garden. Pull your nose from the window and go and find out'.

I had another gawk. He was still there. He was either coming from trouble or going to it, and I knew I'd be the one to blame if we were murdered in our beds so, despite the damp night and my dodgy leg, I pulled my dressing gown around me and out I went.

'Yoo, hoo', I called. 'Who's out there? I said who's out there?'

The bouncing slowed down and as my eyes adjusted, didn't I see a gouger, older than even myself, jumping up and down on Rebecca's trampoline.

'Good evening, sir', he said, in such a polite voice you could tell he wasn't from around these parts. 'If I may be so bold to say, this is a high-quality trampoline. It has put a bit of much needed *je ne sais quoi* back into me'.

'You're damn lucky', I replied, 'I don't have any dogs or I'd have set them on you and that'd give you a bit of jay-ney-whatever, right enough. What brings an oul codger like yourself into my space?'

'Well, I must say it's a calming sort of garden, what with those little solar lights flickering in the flower beds like stars fallen out of the heavens. Seems like a place where a man could gather his thoughts; ascertain his next move'.

'Like robbing a house, maybe? Rifling through our drawers for the last of our treasures?'

'Oh, nothing like that, I assure you', he said in his serious, Sunday-pulpit sort of voice. 'Pray, kind sir, would you not come on up here beside me? Sit with me a while and keep me company. See what I see'.

I was beginning to think white coats and strait jackets.

'Do I not look bad enough, half-crippled as it is without you ...' I started, but he butted in.

'Look, it's easy. I'm not asking you to bounce or anything. Just to see it from my perspective. Here, grab hold of my hand and I'll pull you up'.

So, like a fool, I took in a big slug of night air and let him haul me onto it.

'If that won't be the death of me, nothing will. Just give me a minute till I get my knee working again'.

'See now, that wasn't so bad, was it? He said. 'Just take it slowly as you turn around'.

I did as I was told.

'That's it, let your legs dangle. Now, isn't that just lovely, sitting a little above the ground like this, looking over your garden with the moon above us and flowers not caring whether there's a boom or a bust. They just bloom where they're planted'.

So there I was above on my own trampoline that I had paid good money for with a credit union loan and this chap going on and on about growing and sprouting as if I had never seen my own place before.

'Look', he said. 'Even in the dark you can see the shapes of your daffodils blooming. Over there. Whole clumps of them. Bet they're a glorious sight in the daylight'.

Easy for him to say. He's not the one that has to look after it all. Matthew keeps talking about us getting a smaller place, moving up to Dublin to be beside him but we'd never survive all that light pollution, sirens blasting the place all day long. And it's better for our Rebecca to be able to come to us to see things grow, rabbits in the far field; foxes making their way across the land at nightfall.

'Suppose, it's nice to see the new life coming up, everywhere', I continue and that's when he lets out a sigh.

'New life! Oh … I nearly forgot there for a minute. Coming down I thought the trampoline was like a big black moon that fell out of the sky into your garden and was directing me, helping me to make up my mind'.

'Coming down, is it? What class of drug are you on?'

But he assured me it wasn't anything like that as I sat on the black moon, my legs dangling above the ground, the two of us admiring my own garden as if we were thinking big at the Chelsea Flower Show.

Then he let out a bigger sigh.

'You're like a man who's carrying the world on his shoulders', I said.

'I can't do it, you know. Just can't. The Big Man is asking so much of me this time. I'm getting too old for this job. He doesn't seem to take that into account. When the call comes to jump, there's no two ways about it'.

'Sounds like a bit of a bully to me', I said. 'Could you not just text in sick, take one of them duvet days or pass the job on to some of the younger ones? What about the union? Couldn't you get them on your case?

'Easy for you to say, you're not the one in this dilemma'.

There's nothing worse than a man complaining about his job when he's lucky to have one so I gave it to him good and strong. 'Isn't that better than being one of the hundreds queuing down at the dole office. Not swinging your legs here and feeling sorry for yourself?'

'Ah, don't be so hard on me', he said. 'If only you knew'.

Can't say I'm much good with the sympathetic ear, so I invited him into the house to talk to the wife. 'If anyone can sort you out, it's Dolores. In all the thirty-five years we've been married hasn't she sorted out the world ten times over: Dogs, children, priests, the whole shooting gallery. The ceiling falls out of the kitchen and she's right there with the no-more-nails-solution to stick it back up again. I'm telling you, put her in the Dáil and the politicians would be bringing their sandwiches to work. She'd have this whole bloody recession sorted in the time you'd make a skinny latté'.

I could see he was impressed.

'I'm Jimmy by the way', I said, holding out my hand, 'and yourself?'

'Gabriel'.

So Gabriel and yours truly went up into the house. Dolores was filling her hot water bottle and got all excited when we came in, asking Gabriel straight out why he was dressed up like a kissogram for a hen party and he the age he was. Men don't notice these things but he told her it was just part of the job.

'Mr Gabriel, pull your chair to the foot of the fire and heat yourself. You'll have a cup of something? The kettle, Jimmy!'

While I was getting down the teabags and rinsing out the pot, she was giving him the third degree about what had him wandering around this area. Was he on the run from the police or after breaking out of an asylum, or God forbid, something even worse?

'A banker running from the Financial Regulator?'

'No nothing like that, I assure you. If only it was that simple'.

He gave a big sigh again and she put her hand on his shoulder.

'Don't be upsetting yourself, Gabe, relax. A little nostril breathing'.

'Sorry?'

'Just what you need. Look, follow me. That's it, in one nostril, hold for four and out. And again. Now, isn't that better?'

Gabriel must have been terrified because she had him breathing in and out like a blacksmith's bellows in jig time.

'Now, tell me, Gabe. What is it that has you so bothered?' You can tell us. We won't whisper a word to a soul. Honest to God. So spit it out. Nothing is ever as bad when you whip it out of your head and lay it straight'.

I knew it wouldn't take him long to cave in and I was right.

'In all my life and all the jobs I've done for Him ... this is the hardest ever. I have no way of gauging how it will work out', he started but there was no stopping her now.

'You think life is hard. Look at me. My mother read the tealeaves, told me all those years ago I would marry a man with a wooden leg. Imagine a young girl being told that. I cried my heart out because I thought it would bring me nothing but untold misery, but do you know what? Didn't I get the best man you could ever get. What she didn't tell me was that the wooden leg was made by a carpenter who played the fiddle, that the music in the man's hands went into the leg and now I have a man that dances to my tune all the time. Show him, Jimmy, show Gabe your leg'.

'Leave my leg out of it'.

'Don't be so narky. Now, Gabe, now that you are relaxed, why don't you think of other jobs that you thought were hard and they worked out ok? Take a deep breath. That's it. In your own time'.

And her voice went all soft and whispery.

Gabriel scratched his head.

'I stopped Queen Vashti from appearing naked at the court'.

'From what I heard, well, didn't you do her a great favour. She'd have made a holy show of herself if you hadn't. Anything else?

He let out another sigh.

'Accompanied Mahommed on his night journey'.

'And weren't you the right man for that one, too.

'Had to tell a very old man that his wife was going to have a baby even though she was past her childrearing years.

Dolores was agog with this piece of news.

'No wonder you're exhausted, spreading yourself so thinly all over the world. A bit of you here and a bit of you there, just like that fella, Bono. But I bet the woman was delighted in the end. Sure, aren't they having them up to the age of seventy now and not thinking twice about it. Why are we always afraid to take a risk? Look at Jimmy there. He was afraid to buy the new ride-on lawnmower. He thought the credit union wouldn't give him a loan for it. I just went into them and told them that they couldn't be expecting him to be huffing and puffing up and down that half acre of meadow one leg bockety and the other with arthritis setting in. That soon shut them up. Hold your nerve and take a risk, that's what I always say. Jimmy, get the man a drop of whiskey. He needs more than a cup of tea'.

I went to the press for the bottle. She was still going when I came back.

'Stop stressing yourself; if them bankers can hold their nerve after messing with figures that have more zeros than a dozen packets of Polo Mints then you should have the gumption to hold yours; that's what I always say. A trouble shared is a trouble halved. Now what else did you have to do?'

'I had to tell a young woman that she was to be the mother of God'.

'Mother of God! Oh, the mother of God'. The two of us said together. 'You're joking'.

But he wasn't.

I was reeling but did it faze Dolores? Not one tiny bit and she started talking to him as if she was giving him her recipe for porter cake.

'Well now. Don't you know that your job is the most glorious thing in the world? I'd love all that flying around the sky bringing good news to people who were chosen. Anyone who has been chosen should get down on their knees and be grateful for what they have been given. Sure, any job would be easy after that, now wouldn't it?'

'It's never easy where a child is involved', he had the foolishness to tell her.

She was off again on her hobbyhorse telling him that rearing a child was never easy. About all the mothers who gave birth to kings and murderers and paedophiles and they still did what all mothers do, teach them how to clean their snotty noses, cut up their fish fingers, do everything so they might grow up into good men. That's what mothers always hope. To raise good men.

'Even though it's to do with a child, this one's different; I don't know what will happen after? How one of them will take it?' He tried to explain but there was no winning with her.

'I'm sure if they weren't up for the job they wouldn't be given it, either. Won't they love him from the moment they set eyes on him? Love him no matter what. All parents do. Love their sons above all else. And love them even more if they know there is something different about them. Were you thinking of not telling those people?'

'Well, that's why I stopped at your place. To get the courage to make sure I'm doing the right thing'.

That was a red rag to a bull for Dolores. 'Are you a procrastinator or a prognosticator?' she ordered him. 'Isn't it going to happen anyway. Forewarned is forearmed'.

Before he had a chance to reply, she was off again asking Gabriel to promise her that when he flew in the window in them fancy robes and wings to break the big news to those chosen people that he'd do it right and not leave anyone out.

'Give me your word', she said, 'that you'll tell him, just like you told St Joseph. He deserves that. Give him credit for being a good man'.

Now this is the moment when I wished I could have taken my wife and bundled her into the chest freezer, just long enough to curdle the words coming out of her mouth and freeze them. Because she opened it that bit too far and there was nothing I could do to stop her.

'Look at Jimmy here. Where would I be if he walked out on me three months gone with Matthew and that other latchico, John-Joe Bagnell, having disappeared, like a bat out of hell, as soon as he knew I was late? And here we are now, our son in his mid-thirties, with his fine wife, a house in Alicante, a grandchild that's the apple of our eye'.

'Are you saying what I think you're saying?' I cried out, needing to hear the words out loud or I couldn't believe it. No, I wouldn't believe it.

'Matthew's not my son?

She just looked me straight in the eye. 'But you knew that all along, you must have; what with the colour of his hair'.

The red hair. Why didn't I cop the ginger head? I bet the whole country was roaring laughing at me all these years, the only eejit that didn't cop Matthew's red hair. How did I not see it, the child that I had reared, called my own, would lay down my life for ... he was not mine?

Then she started to argue that I was chosen. 'God knows the right father for a child', she said. 'He always wants the best for his son. So he chose you'.

I wasn't taking that one lying down but she stopped me short, saying that Matthew and me were cut out of one another. All the things I'd done for him. Always cheering him on, whether it was mickey-mouse matches or county finals, it didn't matter. All that good financial advice I'd given him, about pulling out of property ten years ago. And if I wasn't his father, would I have my grand-daughter, Rebecca, my heart's greatest delight, now would I?

She kept going on at me, asking would it have made any difference if an angel had come to me in a dream? Would I have loved Matthew any the less? Would I? What could I say?

I turned to Gabriel for a bit of back-up after me helping him. But he'd gone. Snuck out, by jingo, when I was in the thick of it. Did it matter now? What was at stake here was that Matthew was not my son.

'There was only one minute when he wasn't yours, Jimmy Naughton', Dolores commanded. 'Even less. Bagnell wasn't one for hanging around. In and out like a fiddler's elbow. Think of all the millions of minutes when you have been his father'.

'That's not the point', I said.

She had the last word.

'But it is. Only one minute when you were not. Matthew's your son. It was never any other way. And you were the best father a child could ever have. If anyone was chosen by God it was you. Now, like a good man reheat my hot water bottle for me. I'm off up to bed. And pick up that feather, there, by the door'.

THE CALL

The swans came up into Kieran's garden. They left the lake and stepped onto the wooden pier beside the red boathouse and shook the water from their feathers: the cob, the pen, the two surviving cygnets. They paraded across his grass, ungainly and awkward out of water, before they negotiated the gravel path with their large webbed feet. The two cygnets collapsed every few steps since their legs hadn't yet developed the strength needed to walk on land.

They came to his back door. It had rained heavily all morning and they had sheltered on the opposite shore of the Corrib, but now the sun was shining, so they came late, hitting their beaks off the peeling paint. Brandy barked. It was the signal to his master to get the bowl and soak the bread in water and bring it out to them. They were as much a part of Kieran's life as the dog was. He found the house very lonely at times. If it wasn't for the dog he would have found it almost unbearable to wake up in the morning with no one around since his sister died. Now he had the swans as well. Brandy didn't like them, they hissed at him, their orange beaks as bright as the montbretia that was the only colour in Kieran's garden at that time of year.

'So ye finally decided ye're hungry', he said, as he put bread into the beaks of the mother, then the cygnets and finally the great white male. He was not afraid of them though Brandy sat at a safe distance. 'No wonder ye're so white', he laughed, 'with all that white bread inside ye'.

But it would be the last they'd be getting for a few days. 'I have to go away. My brother Mark on the island, he's not well. It'll be Brandy that'll be lookin' after ye. Won't ya Brandy?' It was just as well there wasn't anyone around to hear him. If there was, they'd have him carted away.

The postman had called to Kieran that morning with a letter from Sarah, his only brother's wife, to say that Mark had fallen and fractured his hip. He was very low. Would he not come visit him? Kieran couldn't remember when he had last seen him. And he didn't want to leave it too late this time, did he? If he had learned anything, it was that. Even if there were big arguments about the hurling and the church, he'd still chance it.

'I'll leave bread out for ye and ye're not to eat it all in the one day. D'ya hear me?'

The swans looked up at him with their black eyes and orange beaks and said nothing. The dog stretched his paws over his eyes.

Kieran banked up the fire before he went down the road to his neighbour, Trish. They were the last two houses on a road that meandered off into the mountain. Some nights he went out walking the hills, his gun under his arm, searching out the fox that came in the lambing season and made off with the best of the newborns. From this elevation he could see across the valley, all the changes since he was a child. All the new houses, talk of windmills. Houses that would have been lost to the landscape then, now had all their lights on. They were like stars that had fallen from the firmament, had landed on the soft earth and still gave off their light. The beam of a thousand candles.

When he got to her house, the outside light hung there from the corner of the gable like a fuchsia flower and lit up the whole yard. Since the night after they buried his sister, Trish had left the light on for him. Every time he looked across the stretch of road to the cottage he could see it shining there. Now it shone on the rain barrel in the corner, on the fertiliser bags that covered the turf, a branch of hawthorn hitting off the stonewall: things that the night's dark robbed from the human eye except when the sky was frosty clear and the moon was full. It was the only sign out there to show that he wasn't on his own on this side of the world.

He should never have let his sister go like that.

Trish came to the door and invited him in. No, he wouldn't go in but if she could bring him to the bus in the morning that would be great. Then he borrowed whatever bit of moonlight came through the clouds till he got back to his own place and brought the dog in from the shed. He let him lie across the hearth, his tail thumping the floor in gratitude.

Kieran left the bread on the step the next morning before Trish pulled up in front of the gate on her way to town. 'Tell your brother he should have married me and not gone off to live on that godforsaken island. If he hadn't, I'd be looking after him now, and he'd be treated like a king'.

Kieran laughed.

'See you when you get back and I'll have this week's magazine for you'.

Trish was a good neighbour. She always brought it to him when she was finished with it. He loved to read the letters from people in America and all over the world looking for the lyrics of songs. He once sent the words of a poem they had learned at school to an old man in Kilkenny and he still got a Christmas card from him every year. And then he had sent the reply to the woman who was looking for a kind man with a sense of humour. Better not to think about that now.

He got the bus that brought him to the pier. He sat on the quay waiting while they loaded all the gear onto the boat: bags of cement, cylinders of gas, a cage with a cat, a camera crew over from Germany who wanted to film the way of life on the place. He watched the island rise up out of the water as the boat cut through the waves.

Regaining his land legs, he walked up the green road past the cliffs and the rabbit burrows to his brother's house. Sarah opened the door.

'Well, aren't you a sight for sore eyes? You'll never guess what the boat's brought in, Mark?' she shouted into the kitchen. They wouldn't mention her letter.

He could have stayed for weeks talking with him about old times, clearing the plates of big dinners Sarah put in front of them. But all too soon it was time to go back.

'I suppose you'll want to go home to your swans, if it's swans you're going back to', Sarah teased as she waved him off at the pier. He was sorry he mentioned them. They would think him a fool.

'Come again', she demanded as he climbed down onto the boat. It was full of students going back to school after their weekend on the island. He had to squeeze himself into a corner while they took over the space with their laughter and their noise and their fancy phones.

Kieran was glad to see his front door. Brandy ran down the path to meet him, wagging his tail in delight, licking his master's hand as he stretched it out to rub the black and white head. He stepped into the hall and felt the cold of the house after the warmth of his brother's cottage. He got some turf from the scullery, opened the door of the range and set a match to them. He let the flame roar up the chimney for a while before he pulled out the damper and the fire settled down to a steady burn.

He opened a tin of food for the dog, then mixing up a bowl of bread and water, he pulled on his wellingtons and went outside, calling as he went into the evening, noticing in the light the first turn of the leaves. He hit the bowl with the spoon; that was usually the signal for the swans to come waddling across the grass. But not this time.

'Maybe they've gone all the way into the city to see their cousins in the Claddagh basin'. But Brandy wasn't listening. He went running down towards the pier barking. Kieran followed the urgency in the bark. There on the water's edge was the bird lying like a white stone, the female and cygnets standing guard around it.

'It's dead', he thought as the water slopped against the pier. The swan didn't move. He knelt down beside it. 'What's up with you, Mister?' He hit the spoon off the bowl again but there was still no movement.

When Kieran looked he saw that its eyes were almost closed. They were swollen and red and green infection oozed from them.

'Look, Mister, we'll have to bring you inside and see what can be done for you'.

The bird made no attempt to struggle as Kieran lifted him into his arms. He weighed a ton. The pen followed quickly behind, the two cygnets falling and stumbling, trying to keep up.

'Sorry, ma'am, but I can't bring you into the house tonight. I'll have to leave you outside while I bring Mister here in'.

He found an old coat and threw it in the corner of the scullery. There was little else in it but old shoes and tin cans, a sack of sticks to start the fire, a shovel. He placed the dead weight of the bird on the coat. Then he went to fill a bowl with water and placed it beside the swan; but it didn't lift its lifeless neck.

Trish came by later that evening with her magazine as promised.

'You have a fine bit of trouble there on your hands. What are you going to do with it? It'll have the scullery destroyed by morning. Would you not leave it out in the shed?'

'It'll be dead if I do that. Do you think you could ring the vet for me?' Kieran had no phone and it was a rare thing for him to ask, but this was an emergency.

'I don't think he's back from the agricultural show yet'.

'What'll I do with him so?' He looked at her, pleading.

'You know there's a fella in town looks after swans. I heard him on the radio. Remember when the oil lorry went into the water and the canal was polluted. He put out an S.O.S for people to come and clean it off their feathers or they'd die'.

'Would you ring him for me?'

'What would you do without me, Kieran Murphy?'

'I'd be dead altogether'.

'We'll have the cup of tea, then I'll go back to the house and ring'.

She returned in a short while.

'I got him all right. He said he wouldn't be out till the morning but to keep the bird warm and if he survives he'll take him back with him and see what can be done. He said not to be too hopeful though'.

He went to bed but he hardly slept a wink. His room was the other side of the kitchen and he left the door open so that he could hear any movement. But there wasn't any so he got up to check if the creature was still alive. There was the last of the heat from the range coming through to the scullery. He knelt by the bird. He had to go very close to it before he could hear its breathing. It was barely audible. 'Just hold on, Mister, hold on another little while, till morning'.

The swan lay on the old coat, lifeless. On the other side of the door he could hear the rustle of its mate's feathers, camped there with her babies.

The sanctuary man came at ten. 'It's a very heavy infection', he said. 'It's all in his eyes, as you can see. I don't hold out any chances for him but you never know. Where's his mate?'

'She's outside the door, was here all night with her two young ones'.

'We'll have a battle on our hands getting him away from her. I'd better bring the van to the front door and get him in before she has the time to attack'.

Kieran helped him carry the great bird out and settle him in the van. Its wheels were on the main road before its family had got around the gable-end of the house. They stood behind the closed gate hissing and spitting. Then they headed down the grass and into the water. Kieran went back to his kitchen.

Three days in a row he went out into his garden. He called and beat upon the bowl but there was no sign of them. Had he lost them all, his family? That's what they were, wasn't it, his own little family? He hadn't realised how much they meant to him. How the ritual of going out each morning and making the sound of the spoon on the bowl had them coming across the grass which gave his life purpose. All that time with his sister and they never spoke. He hit the bowl again but to no avail. They were gone. It was Brandy that got the leftover bread and milk.

He took the bus to the city. He liked to be sitting up high like that, looking into people's gardens, a fork stuck in a ridge of potatoes, chickens scrawbing around cabbage plants. A full line of shirts flapping at the sky.

When they came as far as the Salmon Weir where the bus turned onto the bridge, the cathedral became a shadow against the sky. He wasn't a man for big churches. He often wondered himself why people had to go into such cold monstrosities, thinking God was going to show up when all the time He was outside in the water rushing to the sea or the salmon that fought their way back up the urgency of water to get to where they started out. You didn't get those sorts of miracles in the middle of blocks of marble. Men in high waders cast onto the turbulence and waited to reel in their catch. He wondered, as he did most days, at what point the water from his lake become river and then the sea.

Soon they were turning right at the Town Hall and up by the post office. He remembered when the Garda Barracks was on the corner and the Savoy where he tied his bike before going in to see some horror film with one of those actors he no longer could remember the name of.

Some burger joint had taken it over now.

He let the people off the bus before him and then walked down the town, past the clock that told Dublin Time and looked for the accordion player who was there as long as he could remember. But he was gone and in his place was a young lad with his electric guitar, walloping it away and screeching out at the people who cobbled by. Down past the last of the old shops, the one where he once bought a good suit. A short walk and he was at the Spanish Arch.

He saw them there in the water, all white and mythical as people threw bread into the ripples. The autumn sun glinted off the pink and blue houses on Long Walk. Boats out in the sea. He wondered where Mister was. He thought that the sanctuary would be close by and he would be able to go in and enquire but he suddenly lost his nerve.

He walked along the slipway and watched the swans glide upon the oily water. The gulls were waiting their chance and the bread thrown by the little boy was gobbled by them before the swans got to it. The noise and gabble of them all disquieted him. How foolish of him to come all this way just to be close to the white feathers? It was all he wanted. He thought about his sister. What would she have said if she'd been around? Well she'd have said nothing because isn't that what happened; she had stopped talking to him. All the nights they used to sit by the fire and he'd talk to her about what he was reading. And she loved all the bits of knowledge about the world held between its pages.

He picked up the courage one evening to tell her. About the reply he had sent to the magazine, answering the woman looking for companionship. His sister threw the magazine in the fire and said it would never happen while she was alive. A Maginot line descended upon the house and other than the whistle of the boiling kettle or the clink of a knife on the plate there was no other sound to cash in. They worked and lived, turning hay, clamping turf side by side for nearly ten years, not the breath of a whisper between them.

A hundred times he had walked to the bedroom door that morning when she hadn't come out. He put his ear to the keyhole for the rasp of breath that told him she was still alive. He heard her faint call but did nothing. He didn't go in but went out to feed the calves instead. It was only after he came back and packed sods into the firebox that he took the bike from the side of the shed and cycled to Doctor Hoban's.

They said what killed her was the white walls and the big lights glaring down at her and she never knowing anything but the colour of smoke on the walls and the soft glow of the lamp. When they opened her up they just closed her again with the sound of the nurses' shoes hitting off the marble floor and not a bird singing.

They glided along the water. If his sister saw him now and if any words came from her they would have been that he was a stupid fool and he was going *seafóideach* on them all, doing what he was doing. He'd better be careful. He headed back through the streets, stopping to check if the statue all covered in gold really moved.

That's what he was. Just a foolish old man.

The sanctuary fella came back with the bird at the end of the week. 'It was touch and go for a while but he's a real fighter. He's right as rain again. We've tagged him so we can keep an eye on him from now on'.

He opened the back of the van and the swan flopped down onto the path. The men watched as he made his way across the grass to the water's edge, then slipped through the reeds and swam away.

'What will he do? He's deserted. His family gone'.

'Not for long. If she's still alive she'll come when he calls her'.

'Is that so?'

'Well, listen now'.

The two men watched as they saw the bird swim out into the lake. They listened. Then Kieran heard Mister's call sail across the air.

First they saw the ripples, then the loyal head of the female and the ungainly brown heads of the young ones as they came around the bend of the lake.

Hellkite

Slither of dark under the base of the door sucked out any remnant of light around Doyle's fingers that he stretched out in front of him. He knelt there in the cubbyhole, his knees roaring pain, his heels digging into his arse, his back curved and scourged as if a cat-o-nine-tails was being flailed across it. He lifted up one knee, to give it some ease, cradled it in his palm, until the other one caved in from the strain. So he swopped knees, cradled that one too. How many hours now, his watch sitting on the bathroom window of his flat where he had placed it that morning while he had shaved before meeting her?

He envied it, the night, its ability to come and go as it pleased. Nothing to stop it, no one to tell it where it could or couldn't go as the rain continued to mallet down outside. He could hear it on the windowsill, somewhere on the landing just above his head, that is, if he had his bearings right.

He tried again to shift his body, even the tiniest bit, to get some little ease from the cramps searing down his legs. His feet were bent back against the floor, like the beak of a flamingo grazing algae from the lakeshore. He concentrated on his toes, from the big to the little, mindful of each one as he tried to wiggle them. That set up a chain of pins and needles which finally came to an orgasm of relief. Such gratitude. No sooner had they waned but they started up again. He wouldn't give up, he just wouldn't.

He needed to piss.

It didn't take long for the dark to fill the tiny space he was locked into. He lifted himself from his hunkers and stretched out his hands, inching them forward for the Braille of the fuse box in front of him. He could play a little memory game with himself. How many switches? What was written on them? Get them in the right order: Lights: Upstairs. Downstairs. Cooker. Sockets. All turned down to the ON position, as if electricity was flowing into rooms beyond his reach, lighting them up, occasional lamps illuminating occasional tables at the arms of cosy chairs, a pan searing meat on a halogen ring, the American fridge humming a sinful tune to itself about all the food it held in the cave of its shelves. He flicked all the switches up again into the OFF position. Once more again to ON. It's what she asked him to do, wasn't it? To make sure that the power was coming through when she had known bloody well that there was nothing there to come through.

He shouted out her name, 'Cora, Cora'. But no sound came travelling back. The bitch. Put the 'b' of that in the belly of her name and it was what she was, a snake swaying to its own pernicious music. Stupidly, Doyle had become so distracted by it that it gave her the moment to strike. She had the key turned before he could say, 'Fuck you, Cora'.

No elbow room, cats and swinging no joke, flies an afterthought of dust, rat droppings. He could hear her car pull away, changing gear before she drove out into silence. Whatever way he tried to manoeuvre his limbs, there wasn't enough leverage to get a swing at the door. Even if he could he had heard her pushing something against it. An off-cut of scaffolding, left behind when the builders scarpered, now wedged it tight. A door that he could smash into tinder wood if he was in the right space had left him as helpless as a pigmy shrew when it came down to it.

He tried to stretch, but it only made things worse, pain jumping behind his scull, bringing tears. It reminded him of the time he was in hospital as a child, he was seven, in isolation with the whites of his eyes all yellow and getting sick on the syrupy cherry medicine they forced him to take. There was another boy in a cubicle in the far corner, the curtains permanently curled around his bed. The doctors would come and do something and the boy would cry out. Doyle had imagined them pushing the boy into a corner and forcing his neck down to his knees. He had no idea why he should think that but that's how he felt it must have been. Nothing else would have made his cry carry such agony like that. He cried out himself now for he didn't know which muscle ached more, the one that he could move or the one that he couldn't.

He called again. 'Is there anyone there?' His voice louder and louder in the dark. He stretched out his elbow to connect with the door. Pound it, someone might hear. He tried but there was only a wimp of a thud that fled through the keyhole rusting in the damp.

How long was she going to leave him like this, before her fit of pique shrivelled away? How long was a piece of string? He laughed, a sounding madness in the enclosed space. It was alien to him, hearing his own laughter tumble back against his chest with no one to hear it. Was it any better that he couldn't see the moon keeping itself to itself, flutter of leaves blown in through the broken glass of the windows? Somewhere outside a piece of metal sheeting had come loose and flapped; back and over, back and over as hailstones smashed against it. Thumping him with its frolics. Laughing in the dark, the black humour of that.

'Cora!'

For their children's sake, they had been civil to one another at the parent teachers' meeting, the Wednesday before. They even managed a united smile to hear that Beth was a high achiever whereas Aaron preferred to sit back and watch everyone else work.

While they were waiting to pay over their yearly contribution, Cora had asked him if he would take the children for the weekend; she had the chance to fly to New York with Richard. Doyle didn't want to argue with her so he said nothing for a few minutes, searching around for the words. In all the three years since he became a failed husband how many times would he have been ecstatic to have had his son and daughter for an extra weekend? Having long since accepted that it was never going to happen he had made plans for the coming one. If there was any way to change it he would, but he couldn't, so he explained about someone new in his life now, flights booked, yes, to see Prague. Ellen, her name was Ellen. Maybe another time?

He was relieved how Cora took it. Said she understood; it was short notice after all. Sure she'd get him again.

As they walked across the schoolyard, she had told him about the batch of houses that Richard had bought, dirt cheap, auctioned off because of the state of them. She might have some work for him if he played his cards right. Hanging doors, skirting boards, that sort of thing. Odd jobs. The way she said it, said it all. He would love to have told her to stuff it where raspberries don't grow but beggars and choosers and all that.

Anyway, it was better to keep on her good side, especially after turning her down on the New York business. Last time he tried to stand up to her she decided he could only have one of his children for the designated weekend. She juggled the names in front of him as if it were a choice of beef or salmon, red or white. Aaron or Beth. Beth or Aaron. Oh, she knew what she was doing, all right. There was no way he could do that, pick one over the other. He had always sworn to them that he loved them equally. So he took the only way out he could. He told them he was busy that weekend. They held it against him and cried that his word was not his bond as he had taught them. It was weeks before he got back on an even footing with them again.

'Fine', he had said as she stepped into her car. 'No harm in having a look'. They agreed a time. She said she would pick him up.

They had driven out through the city, onto the motorway. Traffic rumbling to and fro, cars driving to early shifts or leaving behind the late ones, lights on, a claxon of lorries hitting manhole covers on the side of the road. A crow, almost beautiful in its blackness on a bare tree, stretched its corvine wings. It had more colour than the dingy grey all around them, windscreen wipers battling with the rain.

They had turned off at Lucan. She had stopped at a garage for coffee, skinny lattés which she knew he hated, that she slipped into the holders on the dashboard. Letting them cool down, letting the milky scent fill in all around him. Barely taking her foot of the accelerator, she veered onto a secondary road, all pit and potholed. His teeth rattled as she drove right into a crater and gave her tyres an almighty wallop. What did she expect driving like that?

They had pulled into the estate. Richard's new venture. They were well suited: ex-wife and dickhead, his bluster to her breeze. All spit and no polish. Big-bling-things. The bigger the better. The estate was a cliché of all that was bad about the bust. Roads hadn't been surfaced, there were no foot paths. Lakes of water languished in gardens and between paths. For every standing house there were ten that were in ruins, joists and beams curved by the rain into currach ribs. Ghosts leaned out of broken windowpanes of any window unlucky enough to have been glazed. The house she wanted to show him had its porch facing away from the road, its driveway sloping towards the door. Rivulets ran down and lodged in a puddle before the step.

'First job needs doing is that drain, there', he said, just to show he was on the ball. 'Could cause you trouble down the line if the climate keeps changing as it's supposed to?'

'Climate change, bollocks'.

He had looked at her then, the cruel lines etched each side of her mouth. How did he ever marry her? If it wasn't for his children, he would never darken her life again. She had taken so much as it was. He had woken up one morning to discover that he had walked up the aisle that fateful day with his own house, said 'I do' and by the time he turned to walk back down again he had given half of it away.

That stung as much as the ball of fire-pain now stoking his spine from the permanent curve of his neck. He could no longer tell where his legs were on the ground, he could no longer feel them. Phantom legs as if they had been amputated from the knees down but still left with the memory of where they were. He tried to move them side to side to keep the blood flowing but there was no room at all to sweeten even one nano-second of relief.

The mahogany veneer on the front door had peeled away, exposing the white PVC underneath. Opening it they had met a flurry of panic. Tails disappeared into holes in the plasterboard. A dank harvest of fungi, striped and gilled, dropped spores onto bare cement, exposed wires hung from the ceiling. The coffee was beginning to repeat on him.

Once Cora got over her fit of pique, came back, laughing at her little prank and let him out of the cubbyhole, he was going straight to the gym. It would mean a bit more work, more weights but he would practise. He would build up muscles until there were thick and gnarled as tree trunks. Then he would swim the Amazon, powerful in the rush of it, each splash of his arm drawing attention to himself as the killers all around him smelled meat. Dodging the bull sharks, piranhas, malicious logs of crocodiles floating on the surface, while he plundered through the water, evading the giant catfish that could swallow a child whole and come back for his brother. What he wouldn't give for a catfish now, gladly hand her over to it, given half the chance.

Another wave of anger hit but there was nowhere for it to go. Sounds. He shouted out: 'I'm in here'. He listened but there was no response to his call. Only a shuffling like an old man across the floor somewhere outside the cubbyhole, Badger? The house was probably built on the animal's path through fields that they had traversed all their lives, making this their own corridor to wherever they wanted to go until it was swiped from them by the diggers. Well they had the last laugh, didn't they? Repossessing what was truly theirs.

Then a skitter, something scraping at the bottom of the door. It started to gnaw at the wood, tiny incisors eating into it. Not a rat, no, not a rat. A rat would have been able to squeeze in through the tiniest of spaces under the door. The creature scratched away for a while, trying its best to get at him. He could smell it, the vulpine stench of it, reek of damp pelt and viscera. It must have been hungry. It stretched in a paw and tried to dig its claws into the indigo of his jeans. Doyle put his hand down and grasped it. The animal gave out a squeal as it was clenched in the trap of Doyle's grip. It was a vicious little bastard and pushed the other paw which it hooked into the skin of his hand. Doyle screeched back at it. 'Ahhh', and the animal finally scampered.

He needed more than ever to piss.

Cora had never wanted him. In all their seven years of marriage she was only biding her time. She was the one who had walked out after all. Gone off with dickhead in his big vulgar jeep and bull bars. What Doyle failed to understand was that even though she had it all, she just couldn't bear to see him find a little bit of happiness. The way she flattened her neck when she moved her head back was like the poisonous serpent. It wasn't enough that she squirted her venom in his eyes pretending to be charmed, she had to have everything.

Cora.

Bitch.

Cobra.

How she got him into the small cubbyhole under the stairs was worse than the act itself, the shame of falling for it. All she wanted him to do, she had said, was to trip the switch on the meter box in the tiny space so she could check the lights on each floor. Asking him to crawl in to check it, citing her tight skirt and fear of spiders. Him hunkered there, on his knees like a penitent, shouting out to ask which lever it was. She, slamming the door shut. Reinforcing it.

And what would Ellen think when the voice announced the last boarding over the whole fucking airport and he hadn't shown? People bundling themselves into clothes to keep their luggage limit intact while she stood there, her faithful-as-a-small-dog wheelie case to heel as she scanned above chatting heads to see if she could spot him hurrying towards her. Relief brightening her face. He would never ask for another thing, if he could see that relief on her face.

These were pits of houses, ghosts roaming around, going nowhere but in under the stairs. What did Richard think he could do with them? Pigs in pokes. The rain falling down. Why he bought this heap of junk was anybody's guess. A late developer, dickhead described himself to Doyle, with a laugh, when Cora introduced them, saying his name all rolling and simpering. Doyle wouldn't have taken Richard for an eejit. Late developer or no he wouldn't have invested in this heap of shit. And if that was the case then ... She wouldn't have? Would she? Lured him there with the promise of the extra few bob just because she could?

His head nodded and his body gave an exhausted jerk. He could only have dropped off for a few minutes. He woke frantically. His trousers were soaked. He had pissed in his pants. But if he had, he was up to his knees in it. He could feel it soaking through the denim, his runners, in his socks. He lifted his feet as much as he could manage. He slapped his toes onto the ground. A splash. He did it again. Then he remembered what she had said. Flood plain. The blocked drain outside the door, swollen river and rain promised for days to come.

Every Piece of Ivory a Dead Elephant

There are two kinds of people you find at parties; those who don't want to go home, like myself, and those who do. Take Alison and Rob, for instance. See how he caresses the small of her back, inching up her skirt when he thinks no one is watching. She turns around to kiss his mouth, the tip of his tongue touching hers. Then they side-glance their mobiles while they play with their drinks' glasses. He gives her the nod. She lifts her little finger, flicks crumbs from both sides of her mouth, the way women do, careful with her lipstick, before she reaches down, picks up her bag and the excuses start. She has to let the dog out; he confesses to a conference call. He mentions time zones, Hong Kong or Australia and it could be, just could be, plausible.

But I know better.

I top up my wine as they move out into the hallway. He takes her coat from the chock-a-block rack; she stretches out her arms behind her and he glides her into the garment with the mink collar. Then he buttons up his own jacket, with its soft leather that has been chewed inch by inch by a wizened, toothless woman up in the Himalayas. He clicks the car alarm from where he stands in the porch and lights flash across the street before they air-kiss goodnight everyone.

What's left then are the rest of us. Stragglers. Josh fingering the piano near the conservatory, one or two hangers-on leaning over him, as they list out song after old song that they demand him to play. Before I know it, light is beginning to break through the vertical blinds and they are still shouting out that *the winner takes it all.*

I start making myself indispensible, gathering up plates and empty glasses, stacking the dishwasher, asking where I might put the recyclables, anything to save me from facing my cold house.

Beside me is a woman crying in the corner. There is always a woman crying in the corner. She's sitting on the couch, her knees pulled up towards her chin, one glass of wine too many, and all it takes is Josh noodling *the loser standing small* on the keys. The dam bursts inside her and there is no knowing where that will end up, her panda eyes getting blacker and blacker as streaks from her eyeliner run down her face.

It's the final straw for our host. He stands in the middle of the floor brushing his teeth saying, 'Have ye no homes to go to', I tie the tops of the black sacks and heave them into the utility room. Josh pulls the final notes out of the ivories with a flourish before he brings the cover down.

The party's over.

I leave, walk bleary-eyed into the drizzling dawn, reassure them that yes, I'm fine, no, not over the limit, definitely not, and drive around the town for hours just to save myself the loneliness of a silent bed. I take it slowly down the streets, students whooping it up outside Supermacs, the Buckfast buckos chatting to themselves on the square, oblivious to the hard consonants of rain beating off the path. I take the road that brings me out by the college, the roundabouts, past the clinic, onto the motorway and drive until the petrol light starts to show.

Long before I had any inkling that our marriage was over, Phil had begun to move away from me in the bed. The way we slept, the sleep of the spooners, me turned to his back, holding onto him was the way it had always been. I didn't notice it at first or when it started to happen, because everything else still goes on while a marriage is dying. It doesn't die in isolation, you know. Oh, you eat and you sleep. You find the mouldy piece from the back of the fridge and put it out on the bird table before you head off to work, forcing all the cogs into the available holes; you sit down together at the end of the day and thrash out how you might cut back now that your money is no longer elastic. You even lie down beside one another under the same covers and breathe the same air.

At what point he began to move away from me I don't remember exactly but he began to uncleave, shifting his presence a little further each night so that by the morning he was on the other side of the bed. How cold that space became, that arms length of emptiness between us as it grew wider and wider.

When he moved out I couldn't go to the shops any more. I felt eyes on me everywhere as I stood in the queue at the baker's counter for the soft white bread we always bought. Maria bright as a pet summer's day calling to me, 'How's things' and me having no answer to that as she wrapped the soft warm dough in tissue paper and licked the flour from her fingers.

There was the woman at the checkout who put her hand on my arm as she scanned my half pound of butter, my single pork chop and told me how sorry she was. I mumbled something about it being fine and that I was fine. But I wasn't. I didn't even know that people knew.

No one was ever supposed to. I had warned Phil not to tell a soul. Some tiny chink somewhere and the story just found a way to slither out.

People talk. A smidgen of story and they give it oxygen. A spark of gossip gets the breath of air, it blazes; more kindling stories are thrown on it and before you know it you don't have the legs to run free of the flames. I now know that little rumour fires were being fanned up and down the aisles of washing powders and toilet ducks, of diet drinks and fizzy colas. Locals were filling their baskets with low-calorie biscuits and sugar-free cakes. Next morning they wondered why their skirts didn't close comfortably on them? How could they? When they had grown fat on my desolation, whispering that behind every man without balls is a woman who has them in a glass jar on her kitchen counter beside her shining taps and her sparkling sink.

That is until he stands up to her.

Every day after that, when I went out, I learned to zip on my armour, watching like a scared animal in case an attack came from somewhere I wasn't expecting, I was on my toes, awake and alert, ready to run into the bushes at the first sign of confrontation.

I drove out of town to get my hair done, thirty miles this way, thirty miles that. Told the stylist a story of having to meet a client at the main hotel and needed to be looking top dollar. I couldn't take the chance with my local salon, imprisoned under a dryer with my head full of little flags of tinfoil while my highlights cooked and the stylist wheedled stories out of me.

It was a shock at first when I discovered the texts. I scoured the Visa statements looking for further evidence of covert restaurants, one-night not so cheap hotels. But there was nothing, no tell-tale giveaway. I listened to Phil texting in the middle of the night when he was supposed to be in the kitchen heating milk in the microwave for his nervous digestion. I ran through the scenarios of what I would say to him, how I would belittle him, lash him with my tongue and have him come crawling back, begging forgiveness. All I had done for him. I never saw him short for cash when he went for a few pints after a rugby match. I encouraged him to go for interviews when he was settling too cosily into a job, pushing him up the ladder, straightening his tie as he headed out meet his boss to ask for a raise. If it wasn't for me who would he be?

I lay awake and listened to his finger tap away his Morse-code of deceit with more passion in that finger than I had ever known, coming back to bed to sleep like a baby, an arms length away from me and despite the silence of his phone or because of it I couldn't sleep. Tossing and turning, afraid to say anything when it came down to it.

Who would I be without him?

'I'm leaving'. That's what he said standing at the kitchen table, his voice its usual calm self. I was doing that thing that I do; that thing with the rag in the sink. I swished it round the plug hole, my nail cleaning out the grime that gathered in its groove.

'Why?' I asked afraid to look at him.

'It's bad enough that you give me pocket money, finish sentences for me, make me suck up to my boss, or open my letters before I get to them. But you've gone one step too far this time'.

'So what is it then?' I shouted back, 'If it wasn't for me, you'd still be in the warehouse counting pallets of dog food.

'My Avro Lancaster'.

I turned and laughed right into his face. 'That dust gatherer, Airfix paint peeling off the wings. One of the wheels missing. It should have been dumped years ago'.

'You had no right. It was mine, sitting on that shelf in our bedroom all our years together'.

'You're telling me you're leaving because I binned that piece of rubbish', I took out the sink rag and flicked it across his cheek. He didn't even flinch. I watched the red weal surge on his skin. *The loser standing small.*

'That's the last time you'll do that', he said.

He is now happy, living with a woman he had met on the sidelines of the one rugby match that I didn't pick him up from because I was in the dark with a raging migraine. Something in that other woman's eye or the way she tore open the sachet of sugar before she flipped it into her coffee cup and stirred it as they sat in the bar afterwards, obviously stirred him enough to start a conversation and later hold her breasts with the same reverence he held the oval ball.

In all my years with Phil I never got the real scent of his body. He showered every day, put on deodorant and aftershave and I never once remembered how his skin smelled. Before he cleared out all his clothes, finally, I used to go through his wardrobe and put his shirts to my face, trying to get some sense of him, but there was only fabric softener or skin lotion. And when he finally left, there wasn't even the perfume of him to mourn.

Every piece of ivory is a dead elephant: Think of Josh tinkling away on the keys, Goldberg's variations, notes so pure they make water molecules sway in delight. Something had to die to produce that. It is the price we pay for things. The consequences.

The day I met him he was coming out of the car tax office. He stopped to talk. He leaned forward, admired the new cut of my hair, asked me how I was, his usual kind self. But he was different too, taller, his shoulders straight, his head held high. As he went to move away from me I got what I had never got before: the first, ever scent of him. My heart shattered in its cage.

APIDEA

Hilary helped Ambrose choose the new bed only three days before. They went into Mullarkeys and took turns to sit on the edge of each mattress, testing for firmness and comfort, checking out the quality of headboards until he settled on a light oak with a solid base. The shop assistant said the delivery man would be out with it the next day and after they settled on payment, she steadied him on his feet and walked him across the road to the Craven Arms. Since it was coming up to lunchtime and there was lamb on the menu, which ordinarily pleased him, they decided to eat. He was very quiet over his whiskey; it didn't relax him but left him sullen and monosyllabic. He complained about the meat, and told the waiter that serving hogget dressed up as that muck would win the pub no shiny plates on the door.

Days like this Hilary wondered why she did it, his home help: the woman who came in three days a week to clean and cook for him, bring him shopping when he needed it. Days like this, the sky that lonesome grey and he so cantankerous, she resented his daughters with their steel gleam and glass apartments in London and Copenhagen. There they were, immune to his needs in their solar-heated rooms, their blonde children absorbed in their PlayStations and she, the gilly, hauling buckets of coal into a small, damp room while he waited for their conscience-salving phone call every other week.

The waiter brought him another whiskey. She tried to distract him. 'You'll be a lot more comfortable in the new bed, you know. It will be much better for your back and you won't be all stiff in the morning. You should have thrown out that other old thing long ago'.

'You only wanted me to buy a new one because you can have something fancy to lay me out in', he said bitterly and drained the bottom of his glass.

'Don't say that', Hilary replied, 'you know that's not true'.

But there was no talking to him. Five years his carer and God knows it wasn't for the money she was doing it but to try and hold onto the loose end she found herself in after every last thread of her own life had been unravelled. Caring for Ambrose helped her keep a lid on it all when the walls were talking back to her after William's death, the boys now gone. James was working his way to a visa in Perth and David was causing a rumble in Christchurch. That part of a woman that needs to be minding someone was crying out for a cause and she jumped at it when the agency rang her. There were times in the last few months when his humour was so bad she could have easily packed it all in, but on good days when he wasn't as prickly as a blackthorn bush she had a real soft spot for him.

That fondness started way back. What was she but a gawky teenager, all buck-teeth and belligerence and no pleasing her, according to her mother.

She was rushing in from school, slamming the gate against the wall and making her mother jump as she stood at the door polishing the brasses. What they heard first was a slow hum. Then it got louder as they saw the black cloud coming down the street. Her mother called out to Mrs Ransome who was pulling the shade over the Communion frocks in her shop window to save them from discolouring. She saw it, too.

Hilary tumbled after the cloud. Blind Billy's dog, knowing it was time to take the turn for home, picked up the sound and stopped in his tracks, while she called out to Tim Forde coming out of the hardware shop with a new cylinder for his Superser. Then she ran to Mrs Meeney who was sweeping laburnum flowers from her path.

The commotion grew louder as Hilary stuck her head into Pottle's Snug where Tom Pottle was putting a cheese and tomato sandwich in his fancy new toaster. The Dolan twins were sitting at the counter, their fingers wrapped around their soothers. 'Come quick', she shouted and dragged them out into the street.

The swarm by now had landed on the handlebars of Mick Maloney's bike, a dark thunder ball of bees hanging onto the metal. Some onlookers were alarmed; others were enthralled, forgetting the stew on the range, cattle to be fed, a lonely voice talking out of the television to an empty kitchen and not a child in the house washed.

Mesmerised, they all stood staring at the insects crawling over one another, a sphere of humming and buzzing, biding their time until the scouts who had flown ahead to check out a new colony would dance their way back. Someone sent for Ambrose Farrell. He arrived covered from head to toe. His movements slow, measured, unthreatening; they watched him pluck handfuls of crawling sibilance up with his hands as he sought out the queen, full of beebread and royal jelly. He did this again and again until he found her, bigger than the others, though now slimmed down to fly and he placed her in the makeshift cardboard hive. That was all that was needed to coax the workers from the bike and, like umber liquid from a jug they poured themselves into the box. He moved away with them then and the street returned to itself.

But Hilary didn't. Something about his movements calmed the urgent buzz inside her. And she felt quieter, so much so that her mother wanted to take her to the doctor to see if she was coming down with something.

Next day she rushed home from school to his place beyond the trees where the hives stood on their base blocks. She crept to the corner of the hedge and hunkered down to watch him through the branches. And there he was, dressed like an astronaut, smoking them out, quietening them, his big-gloved hands reaching in to find the comb, working calmly around the seething insects, removing it. She didn't know that he was aware of her until he came across the field and handed her a piece of honeycomb. How magic that first taste of sugar and wax as she sucked the bee-ness from its walls.

After that there was no stopping her. Almost every day if her mother was looking for her she knew where to find her. With the beeman. His own daughters had never shown an interest in his madness, as they called it, and had flown as soon as they had qualified from college.

He had found an old suit for her, so big she looked like something that had shrunk in the wash. He helped her into it, fastened it up so no insect could get in. She peered out through the mesh as he took the crown off the hive and lifted out a frame. It was a heaving crawl.

'Does your mother not know she'll have to clip your wings if she wants to hang onto you, otherwise you'll fly like the queen bee?' he was forever telling her.

How did it happen that she stayed, never flew. She and William could have gone, should have gone, when they had the chance. Toronto, when the company shifted back after the tax exemptions dried up. They could have reared the boys to the sound of sprinklers misting the lawns, autumn flashing through the Rouge Valley, snowploughs on the 401. But her husband was not for shifting, better to rear the boys on home ground, even if he was redundant. Sure they went anyway. All of them.

'You're not listening to me', Ambrose complained and his lonesome voice pulled her back into the dark hub of the bar where he was putting his hands into the sleeves of his coat.

'A bag of weasels would be a better companion than you', she said as she gathered up his bags.

'When did I become your companion?' he retorted, and agitated, Hilary guided him towards her car at the corner of the street.

He only got one night in the bed. When she went in the following morning she found him on the floor, the bedclothes pulled on top of him, the hard mattress giving in to no one. She could just about make out the pulse in his neck as she called his name. But he couldn't talk and she sat holding his hand while the ambulance raced along the potholed road towards them. He opened his eyes. She could barely make out the words. 'You have to tell them'.

'Don't be silly', she said. 'You're not going anywhere. The doctors will have you as right as rain in no time so save your breath to give out to me'.

'Promise me', he repeated before they put the mask on his face.

'Ok, so'.

'Say it'. But the paramedics were out the door before she could answer him.

As she put her head around the door of St Anne's Ward she knew that his instinctive reaction would be to raise his hand to cover his face. Still with pride intact he did not want anyone, to see the embarrassment of tubes that came from a machine at the side of the bed and carried to his lungs the oxygen that he could not draw himself. He lay there against the starched, squeaky pillows and rubber sheets while nurses busied themselves around the floor, adjusting drips, checking blood pressure. A television told the sleeping patients that the bankers were acting like high-octane movie stars calling the shots, shooting the messenger. He looked small and vulnerable in his hospital pyjamas.

She tried to distract him with a programme she had seen on the nature channel some time back. A man chopping a foothold into a tree and skimming up the bark like a simian, carrying with him a brace of smoking leaves. He waved the smoke in front of him as he plunged his hand into the dark cloud that buzzed all around his thin, brown body. 'Empty your heart of fear', was what the man said, 'and you won't fall' as he lifted out the liquid luxury and put it into his basket for his wife waiting down below.

'Remember', she had said trying to jog his brain back to its earlier sharpness but there was no reaction from him. She talked about the little box for rearing the queen, where he put fondant in the special food place, took a mugful of nurse bees from the bucket and poured them into the mini-hatchery waiting for the queen to grow.

'What did you call the box again? she had asked him. Testing him, testing herself. She actually couldn't remember. There wasn't a meg out of him so she didn't know if had heard her or not. She stood, ready to sneak out.

'Don't forget to tell them', was all he said.

On her way home she went by his house to check on it. Nipper was still in the same spot by the gate where he was when the ambulance took his master away. He followed her car in the driveway, came wagging to the door expecting to see the beeman get out the passenger side. She could feel the dog's breath on her legs as she rang the man's daughters, explained it all to them, the fall, the ambulance, what the doctor said. Their tone was cold as if it were all her fault. As if she were the incompetent daughter that they could expect nothing more from. Agnes would have difficulty getting a flight, she told her, and one of Kitty's sons had an Irish dancing *Feis* coming up and they would have to wait until that was over.

As if an ailing heart would wait for the final dance when it wanted to go somewhere else? When it was being called to go somewhere else.

Spitting anger at them, she gathered up the swaddle of clothes that were in a mound on the two-seater by the fire. Underneath she found the remains of his last job. He had been engrossed in this new task for a few weeks now. His gauntlets and veil on the table, as well as broken pieces of honeycomb, knives covered with wax from his earlier work of de-capping. She took down a mug, added a spoon of cider vinegar and honey, poured on some boiling water, stirred it. She held the warm drink between her hands. There was safety there in that bee space, that tiny cell of warmth and comfort.

She had asked him that day what he was making. She had never seen one before and he explained it to her. A skep.

'Do people use them still?'

'They don't really, but there's a Victorian garden in Cornwall that wants them. That is if I can come up with the proper thing. I haven't made one myself since the girls were small. You know the way everyone wants all the old things nowadays. Hen arks this week, donkey carts, allotments, knitted *geansaís*. Anyone would think we never had a tiger roaming around the countryside for the last ten years. What is the saying ye young ones have, old is the new, new'.

'So you consider me a young one now do you', she said with a smile.

'Well compared to me, Queen Bee', he continued as he handed her the bramble. 'Look, hold this for me while we bind the straw with it'.

'Like this?'

'Yes, now pull on it a little tighter. Do you know, you're as handy as a little pot?' That was the biggest compliment he had ever paid her.

She took the unfinished wicker hive and brought it with her back to her own silent house. She switched on the television to draw some life into the walls, each programme more disheartening than the other. She flicked from channel to channel trying to find something that would fill the empty space inside her. She thought of the man bringing honey to his wife. How advanced a heart that man was, she thought, to know what his wife wanted and got it for her. William hadn't that sort of advancement. How quickly the sweetness between them turned to bitterness of disappointment as the years went on. So many losses in her life, so many leavetakings, and if Ambrose went ... She couldn't bear the thought of it. It was what she needed to do herself: Empty her heart of fear and she wouldn't fall.

They came back in time to see him laid out, back in their old home again as if they had never left. She made them as welcome as she could, freshened up beds for them, wet the tea, stopped herself from saying anything to Agnes when she took down the painting of the pheasants to search it in case there was a wad of notes secreted in its backing. Nor did she say anything when Kitty remarked on the waste of good money the new bed was with its white embroidered linen that Mary Walshe had lent her.

There was a steady murmur of talk in the kitchen, along the hall, the constant sound of footsteps at the door. He wouldn't be cold in the ground when they would start clearing things out, a skip in the garden, neighbours whipping things out of it at night that they would find good use for. But not this trumpery, his suits, his gloves, his apidea. Now she remembered, that's what he called it, his little queen hatchery. So many bees reared in it, sent to beekeepers all over the country. Who would rear his queens now?

Mrs Meeney came blustering in to whisper that Father Timmons had come. He stood there in his grey cashmere jumper, black shirt and trousers. Someone went and turned down the volume of the television. Ambrose's words were ringing in her ears. 'It falls to you', he had said.

She was superfluous to requirements. So she left him in the presence of the priest and went out the back door. A few men were leaning against the porch smoking and sorting out the global crisis. She opened the small gate that led down through the orchard to the far wall where the hives were kept. The sun was low in the sky and would be gone before long. It spread its last shadow-beams along the garden. There were a few straggler bees still mooching around outside the hive. Flying in with baskets laden with pollen, a few dead insects on the old bit of carpet he had under the plinth of the hive. A low murmur within.

She felt awkward and stupid, but a promise was a promise. He had told her what to do, to rattle the bunch of keys, place some spice cake and sugar before the hive.

'Bonny bees, bonny bees, hear what I say'.

She had laughed at him then, his *pisreogs*. He had asked her to do this, to tell them that he was dead, so that they wouldn't swarm, wouldn't fly off somewhere else.

But what was the point in them staying? Who would mind them, now that their master was gone; no one to look after them when winter came? No one to clip the queen's wings.

She hadn't actually promised in the end. That moment before the ambulance took him away, she hadn't said the word, so she wouldn't be breaking her bond.

She turned and walked away from them, stopping a safe distance. The murmur began to build, louder and louder with great urgency as they began to pour out of the hive.

Backmasking

Heat fell down through the night as Kev made his way home from the wall. Before he even got to his house he could make out the shape of his da sitting on the doorstep. Kev sat down beside him as close as he could without touching him. Patches of sweat leached out of his shirt like lost continents newly discovered.

'Locked out again?' he asked.

Stars exploded and disappeared into black holes in the time it took his father to reply.

'You know your mother, son'.

Kev wasn't sure what to say to him so he stuffed his hands further into his pockets.

'What she on about now?'

'She doesn't mean it. It's not a barrel of laughs for her either. It's this frigging weather and the bills don't go away, you know. If a job doesn't come soon ...' And his voice sort of trickled down the plughole of the dark. They sat there for a while watching the light fall from the street lamps and the night creep out from under the hedge that divided them from the neighbours. Kev began to yawn. If they sat out there any longer they'd be turned into pillars of sleep. His da smelled of pigeons.

Kev crouched down in front of the door, pushed open the letterbox and shouted through its gaping mouth.

'Ma, it's me, your darlin' son. Let us in'.

He had to call three or four times before he heard her come squeaking along the hall in her baskety sandals, the only ones that would fit her swollen feet. 'Puffer-fish feet' his sister, Saoirse, called them.

His ma opened the door.

'My two great men', she said, as she stretched out her hand and flicked the ash from her cigarette onto the step beside where his da was sitting; he brushed off the dust that landed on the sleeve of his shirt, stood up. He had walked by her, through the house and he was out in the yard by the time Kev got to the kitchen.

His ma stuck her feet back in the basin of dead-sea salts. 'They're even bigger than yesterday', she barked out at her husband as if it was his fault her feet had swelled up. From the window Kev watched his da look up at the roofs of the houses waiting for his life to change.

Then he went up to bed to the dark, the quiet blocking out his mother's shouting that if he came home from the wall that late again he could sleep out with the da's pigeons for all she cared.

There was no set time for the wall; they just turned up, Kev, the three lads, the two girls. It was that simple. Once dinner was over, he took the stairs, two at a time, up to the landing window to watch for them. Damo came first, then Creeper, usually followed by Jacinta and Natalie. When he finally caught sight of Atlas loping along, carrying the world on his shoulders, he took the stairs in reverse and out the door, his ma roaring after him not to take it off its hinges or she'd have his guts for garters.

The wall was around Mrs Feeney's garden. It was the only detached house on the corner of River Oaks, a mad name for a road that had neither water to cool them nor trees to shade them from the crazy heat that loaded itself into the furnace of concrete and blasted it out day and night. 'The hottest summer in years', the telly said.

Mrs Feeney didn't seem to be too bothered by the gang of them taking over her wall. Once or twice they saw her in her back garden pinning clothes on the clothesline but more often than not she was hidden behind her sitting room curtains that stayed pulled to stop the sun from fading her furniture. Her cat, though, commanded the window sill, stealing the limelight, as if he was about to pronounce the next date for the end of the world from his cat lips. But all he did was lick his fur, settle into his regular, sleeping pose.

They let him get on with what cats do best while they had a beano, swapping football cards or arguing about who scored what on 'Match of the Day'; who sang best on 'Top of the Pops'. Natalie had a thing for Kev. She pretended to be one of the lads, just so she could arm-wrestle with him, asking to see his muscles. Kev couldn't bear her going on like that and tried to ignore her. When he did, she'd frump herself on the wall with a big puss on her, her cheeks red from exertion and the heat. It was up to Jacinta to try and cajole her back to herself, twirling her hair and tying it up with bobbin thing-a-ma-jigs until she settled back down again.

He felt bad about that.

Damo brought along his guitar. He had got it as a birthday present from his gran. He was living with her since his mother pulled out her own front teeth because they were telling her to take a lump hammer to his father.

Damo was as harmless as a bee in butter; hadn't a clue about music but that didn't stop him. The pads of his fingers were raw from the practising and after weeks he had mastered the first few chords of *House of the Rising Sun*. He'd start real low and soulful ... *there is a house* ... standing there on the edge of the path and then his voice began to croak, but he'd keep on, forcing the notes out. Creeper joined in, bringing his own voice down into his boots and Damo stripping the skin off his finger pads he was strumming so hard, the heat getting to him, the rest of them joining in at the bottom of their voices ... *way down in New Orleans*.

When Damo got the hang of that he started ... *tell me why I don't like Mondays*.

Kev wasn't sure when Jason Lawless started to come sniffing around. At first he just sat there at the edge of the wall, chewing his nails, saying nothing. He was older than the rest of them, a shadow of dark on his upper lip. Atlas who never wanted to be the centre of attention went a bit loopy and started acting the smartass. He grabbed the guitar from Damo, being Jimmy Hendrix, turning the instrument the wrong way round, strutting up and down the road as he pretended to be working the stage. He was nearly upended himself when Mrs Egan took the corner too fast in her little blue Corolla and he had to jump up on the path before his feet were taken from under him. When he handed the guitar back to Damo his face was all red. Jason Lawless sat there, chewing his nails and sneering. Kev couldn't stop looking at him.

Later he walked back home with Jacinta because she lived in the estate just behind his. The lads slagged them, 'we know what you're after', but there was no chance of that. Ever.

All the houses had their windows open trying to let some air through. Mary Thomas was walking up and down her path with a bawling baby. He was covered in prickly heat; she was shushing and shushing him on her shoulder trying to get him to shut up. Jacinta said, as she was going through the gap in the wall, that Jason Lawless made her feel the way she does when she sees a rat scuttling out of a hole with its squirmy tail and knowing face.

Kev let on he agreed with her.

'He's a chill waiting for a spine to run down', she said. 'He has the creepiest hands I ever laid eyes on. Did you see the state of his nails? There's nothing left of them with all the chewing he's done on them. A devil gnawing his own flesh'.

'Sure that's no crime', he said, wanting to defend him, not telling her that what he had noticed were his arms. Compared to the rest of the lads whose skin had been burned over and over since the heatwave began, Jason's were pale and skinny, like when an old plank of wood was turned over and there underneath would be a weed, all anaemic white, trying to grow without light.

In his bed, the clothes kicked off, Kev couldn't sleep from the heat and the image of Jason's hand as it rose to his mouth to chew another nail, the curve of a snake curling down his forearm into the valley of his elbow. Next day he was late for school. Mr Dolan shamed him once again, calling out 'You, Ryan. What excuse is it this time?'

'Pssss!' he could hear under the breath of the others around him. He didn't care because he kept telling himself it was Tuesday and by Friday he'd be fecking his school bag into the cubbyhole under the stairs and he wouldn't have to worry for months about why he didn't like Mondays.

They forgot about Jason. Week after week they settled into their holiday ways. Damo had a little routine going for himself by now, starting with *Rising*, then *Don't like*

Mondays and sometimes he'd throw in, *The Boxer*, just so they could all *la la la* to the chorus, while Creeper would add his ssswish of percussion.

Damo was peppering to go straight into his finale. After weeks of finger-picking and blisters he had mastered the first few notes of *Stairway to Heaven*. He stood in front of the rest of them on the edge of the path, his red hair a flame around his forehead, his cheeks a mottle of freckles and with a croak, broke into song. Kev and Creeper followed. Then everyone else joined in the chorus, even Atlas. *Oh, it makes me wonder.* The girls were mad about that bit, *oohing* away into their hairbrush microphones.

Damo wanted them to start a band. His gran said they could have the shed out the back; they could get drums, another guitar maybe; there was talk of a synthesiser. He'd even let the girls in. Backing singers.

'And maybe we could have scumbag as our manager'. Creeper said under his breath, indicating the figure coming from the far road, along by the shops, the sun a searing ball as it fell between O'Grady's and Mullin's side entrance. Jacinta stopped singing the chorus, then Natalie. By the time Jason Lawless reached the wall, Damo was going solo. Atlas started to get jittery, picking at his eczema on the insides of his wrists until it was real angry and weeping. The girls started measuring up the size of their hands. Creeper started creeping back into himself.

Lawless sat on the wall. A Daddy-Longlegs came from under the capping stones and crawled along the top. Jason put his hand out on the cement and let the insect climb along his fingers into the palm of his hand. It stretched along his forearm; he turned his hand over and watched it walk down the other side. Then he picked it up. He stretched out each long filament of leg. Without a blink he pulled off each of them, one by one and dropped them on the ground. What he was left with – a grey little egg of a body – he flicked like a piece of nose jam into the road.

They looked at one another trying to read each other's faces. None of them spoke. Damo and Creeper started to laugh because they didn't know what else to do.

Then Jason said, 'You're singing that song wrong way around'.

They hadn't a clue what he was talking about.

'If you knew anything you'd be back-masking it'.

None of them ever heard that word before but Jacinta wasn't going to let him get away with anything.

'We all knew that'.

'Tell us so what it means if you're such a clever bitch'.

'It's for me to know and you to find out'.

Kev looked at Jacinta and she suddenly became very interested in the split ends of her hair, like she was counting each strand. He watched Jason where he sat at the far side of the wall with his pale arms and his dark eyes looking out from the hood of his hair.

'You're bluffing', he continued.

Then he started singing mad stuff about Satan or something, lines that made no sense, swinging the words backwards as he jumped down off the wall and wandered off into the night, down past the shops, the video hut, the chemist and the mini-supermarket, past Damo's gran's house, his Jesus-striding-into-the-desert hair flowing behind him as he sang.

'What was that all about?' Kev asked Jacinta as they wandered home.

'Haven't a clue', she said, 'but I wasn't going to let on to that asshole. I'll look it up in the dictionary as soon as I get to my room'.

Kev knew there was little chance of him doing that. Some houses live by the bible others by the dictionary, theirs was neither. 'There's no money in words', his da always said, 'Mose's or anyone else's'. There wasn't much money in anything according to him. The best use of newspaper he said was to put it under his pigeons to collect their crap. Now that his job had gone in the paper mills he was spending more and more time out the back with them. Kev's ma said that she could see downy feathers growing around his ears.

She was in the kitchen making sandwiches for an Oriflame party. Kev asked her what back-masking meant but she told him not to be annoying her. Then he asked her if they had a dictionary. She pointed to the box with her bits and bobs under the telly. Above it hung the Pope's blessing, well faded by now, there since they got married. It had been read out at their wedding reception, she told them once. Saoirse said 'a fat lot of good it did them' and she got the whip of their mother's hand for that.

If a dictionary was anywhere it was going to be there among her Novena books, her medical card and old bingo cards with the numbers all marked off in blue marker. He pulled them out but all he could find was the *English-Irish Dictionary* that Saoirse made their ma get for her when she went to Irish College. It didn't do her much good and she got a big duck egg in her Inter-Cert the next year. She was a Redcoat in Butlin's for the summer so Kev didn't have to put up with her screaming matches or her calling him 'perv' all the time.

The word wasn't there in Irish or in English.

His da was out the back. He stood there, St Francis of River Oaks, listening to the wind-clap of wings as they flew down to him. Smiling. The Devaneys next door were always fighting with him because of the way the roof of their house was shat on by the birds. It got so bad once they reported him to the health services saying that the grain was drawing rats into their garden. They had little rockeries here and there and the pigeons dropped grain all over them. Stray grain fell in between the stones and Kev thought it was like a parable straight out of the bible because some of the seed sprouted and long green sheaves of corn shot up between the purple-yellow granny faces of the summer pansies. The Devaneys were livid. 'How they have time to notice pansies is anybody's guess', his da said, 'and them working every hour God sent?'

'Da', Kev called, but his father didn't hear him, or if he did, he didn't let on.

He shouted again.

When he turned, Kev saw the way the smile went back to where it came from. As if his son's voice reminded him of how easily the gates of heaven could shut.

'Do you know what back-mask ...?' and then he stopped. He remembered when the man from the health services came to investigate. He had a face on him like someone who hadn't enough roughage in his diet. As he filled out the report form his da lost the rag with him and said the birds weren't doing anyone any harm. Where did the neighbours think they were living, having a garden with its cutsey, windey path that curved up to their wooden shed with roses falling down over the doorway?

'Straight out of *Little House on the Prairie*', he shouted at the man from the health services. Did they not know they were living in a housing estate?

'It's fierce hot; isn't it, Da'.

'Tis, son'.

Kev went back in and waited for sleep, waited for the first faint note of the birds that he'd miss if he didn't listen very carefully, hearing the *coo coo coo* that finally blocked out the word that Jason used. By morning it had faded from his memory.

The weather held for those weeks and the light went on and on in the evenings. Their arms and legs were getting browner by the day. Anyone that had cars went off to Brittas Bay or Clara Lara Fun Park and didn't return home until well after the road was silent. Atlas went to his aunt's mobile home in Curracloe, Creeper went camping to Enniskerry and Natalie went off to Fuenguerola with a face on her as long as a wet week because there wasn't rain lashing off Mrs Feeney's wall when she was saying good bye to them.

They were down to just Damo, Jacinta and him.

That night the heat was no different. The pigeons were listless on the back fence. Before he went out, his ma was complaining of a thunder headache and lashing out at his da that something would have to give soon or she wouldn't be able to go to the Embankment. As if his father could bring on storms.

Damo was kicking the wall with his foot and for the want of something better to do Kev picked up the guitar and started to try out a few chords.

They were edgy enough as it was and when they saw Jason Lawless head towards them, sucking all the heat out of the air in front of him, he felt Jacinta shiver. As he came closer Kev shivered, too. He stood on the edge of the footpath, leaning into them and then away from them. He moved and sat on the wall beside Damo. Nobody said anything. Mrs Feeney's cat came along the path for its nightly stroll. It jumped up on the wall and stroked itself against Jacinta. She rubbed his tiger head. Jason leaned across to her and picked it up. He put his hand on the cat's back and started to rub its fur the wrong way. The cat hissed and arched its spine. It tried to struggle out of Jason's grip but he held it in the vice of his arms. He caught the cat's head, pulled it back in the way you would when you're trying to get worming tablets down it.

'Bet you thought I was going to do something awful to it?' he said looking directly at Jacinta.

'You wouldn't …?'

'Wouldn't I?' and before Jacinta could answer he stretched out his hand and bent the cat's front paw backwards. They heard the splinter of bone. The cat yowled blue murder as its other claws speared into Jason's hand. 'Fuck it'. His grip lost its hold; the animal struggled for a few seconds, catapulted out of his arms and hobbled back into the garden.

Jacinta screamed 'you evil bastard' and threw her sandal at him. He ducked.

'At least one of you has balls, I'll give you that', he sneered at her. 'More balls than any of the pansies here. A girl with balls, I like that'.

Licking the blood from his hand he slipped from the wall and wandered off again into the night heat singing under his breath *here's to my sweet Satan*.

They watched the cat crawl away, in behind the neat rows of blocks stacked on the foundations of the new garage that Mrs Feeney's nephew was building for her. They could hear its low pitiful mewl as it tried to find a place to hide itself. Jacinta was still crying when they walked back home.

He found his da in the back garden. The birds were all around him, their plumage puffed out, their tails fanned. Some of them had beautiful wing patches shining in the evening light, a pink iridescent sheen as they pecked away while his da stood there, a smile on his face like he wasn't worried that his job was gone or anything; like he was seeing the gates of heaven open before him.

Kev stood at the door, waiting.

'What is it son?' he said.

'Did you ever wish you had a different life?'

'That's an awful big question so late at night. What has you asking me that?'

'It's just ...'

'If', he said, 'if I didn't have this life, I wouldn't have had you and where would I be then? Whatever way you say it, it always comes back to that. Now be off to bed before your ma gets back'.

Then he did a strange thing. He put out his hand and touched his son.

Kev couldn't remember him ever touching him before.

He was still awake when his ma came home and she must have had a few glasses of wine because she was loud and pleading with his da and he kept saying 'no'. Soon there was enough snoring coming from their room to shake the dust from the mattress as Kev lay on his bed.

All he could think of was the way Jason looked when his pale arms were wrapped around the cat, back-stroking it, and how his tongue licked the blood off his scratch. He got a shiver when he thought of his arms around him, how cruel they could be, how sweet.

Foraging

When it comes to women I'm as helpless as a cow in quicksand. I just let them keep breaking my heart over and over. Angie has a real battle on her hands trying to put her Humpty Dumpty back together again. But she's fighting a losing battle.

She had given me a gift voucher for night classes, a surprise for my helium balloon birthday: *Beginners Guide to Avoiding Adultery*. The problem was that I fell head over heels for the tutor with her long, leisurely legs and pouty, luscious lips. I probably wasn't the sharpest knife in the drawer to ask Angie to renew my subscription for another few sessions; especially when I came home one evening with lipstick not just on my collar, but on my receding hairline and the tip of my ear. She simply saw red.

Before I knew it she had piled my clothes into plastic bags: shirts, jocks, shoes, toothpaste and lined them up at the door. Then she pinned the note to them. She had chosen her words well.

I was out on my ear. It was only then it dawned on me you could never know a woman any more than you could the black hole I was falling into. But I knew enough to realise that without her my heart had nothing to hold it together. It started to lose its sticking power and before I could say dumb-ass I was slumped on the doorstep, my face sunk into one of the black plastic bags and the *nee-naw nee-naw* of the ambulance screeching its way through the narrow streets to our house.

That was enough to bring Angie running back. I had done the damage good and well. There was no choice for the surgeon but to shuffle his tarot cards and in triumph selected a transplant that most suited my personality. He sawed through my sternum, opened me up like a ziplock bag and plucked my broken heart from between my ribs. Angie had called me heartless and that's what I was just for a short time until my new model was nestled into its cavity and the blood pa-thumped, pa-thumped again through my arteries.

When I woke up I was beside my old self in the starched, white bed. Through the haze of opiates, her meerkat eyes were peering down at me. Her caramel wrappers made a racket as she sat there pulling the papers off the sweets and popping them into her mouth. She had been holding vigil by my side for the dark and light of two whole days and when she saw my head move she gave a little skip of excitement. This dislodged my drip and the world and its mother of buzzers started buzzing.

'My Lazarus is back', she started to sob, the caramel swirling around her chubby Angie cheeks. If I wasn't such a down-to-earth kind of a guy I would swear I was levitating, nose to stipple with the ceiling.

'Blah de blah de blah', she continued as the nurse came running down the ward, shoving lights into my eyes and asking me ridiculous questions about who I was and what day it was.

'A bishop wouldn't ask me that', I slurred.

'I'll let that go this time', Angie complained. 'All that matters is that you're back to me'.

'I wouldn't bet on it', I said. 'Someone's back, but I'm not sure it's me. It's not often you'll see a sheep breakdancing'.

'What?' she said. But before I could make sense of my own words I fell back into the arms of Morpheus and dreamed a dream like all the great men of the world. Zillions of euros running around the field were just sheep droppings that bankers and bondholders stepped on and flattened into zeros. If Angie had asked for a new man, she was getting one.

I had arisen.

In no time I was back home. I grew nose hairs. I started to go out walking. Our canary became my little feathered companion. I perched the bird at the end of a broomstick, piled a maum of grain into my pocket and we sauntered down the street. The bird gave a little every-so-often tweet at the end of the handle where it perched, all orange and yellow with a fine blue head on it. When someone stopped me I poured a measure of seed into the other person's hand. The bird skipped from the handle to the palm of the stranger and pecked away. Women especially were delighted. They danced a little jig there and then.

All this new energy was now in my body and the blood still going pa-thump through the tiny tunnels of my system.

When the dreams started to come I wasn't so scared at first. Angie tried to reassure me. 'There's nothing like the chunk of smelly Gorgonzola to make all hell break loose', she said though that didn't settle me one little bit. She just stared at me with her slippery, dippery eye like she was looking down the wrong end of a telescope.

I was left with the feeling all day long. Even when I walked down the street, the bird chirping away on its stick and distracting the traffic wardens from sliding big fines behind windscreen wipers, I kept looking behind. But there were just ordinary women tottering on heels, an old man pushing himself with a walking stick, a dog smoking a cigarette beside a dust bin.

I started lingering at vegetable counters. While Angie was in a sweat-dither as to whether she wanted to feed me slim-line or skimmed milk the smell of cabbage leaf sent me into a gallimaufry of ecstasy. I could sniff out lettuces a mile away. I craved the green of chlorophyll. Little Gems, Cos, Romaine, in their gloriously-wilted existence brought pleasure to my lips, my throat, the soft parts of my mouth that no one else knew. They looked so delicate all bunched up there it took every iota of my resolve not to push my face into the bosoms of them.

Next day when Angie was cooking up a big pan of rashers the smell drove me out of the house and across the gravel to the corner of the garden where the shed stood. Over the years it had become the Park Inn for all the useless things that Angie bought on eBay, but never once saw the light of day:

a set of fire extinguishers used only once
drawers that had no chest of
a set of matching dog leads

Up and out with everything; into the skip I ordered the day Angie went off to the consultant to see how she could get her old man back. There was as much chance of that happening as there was of getting a hen to tell the truth.

Enough scrap was piled up to make a hawker rich as I threw the last of the three barbeques on the mound. The floor at last was able to take centre stage so I unrolled the sleeping bag, fluffed up the pillows and made a cosy, little bed-space for myself in the corner. When Angie came back I could hear her going around the house calling me, out through the garden, my name swinging on the wind. Oh, I didn't answer, just sat there admiring the tiny view from the window as the Buena Vista Social Club jammed away on my MP3 player. Finally, I heard her stop outside the door.

'Lazarus, are you in there?'

'Go away', I said.

'Don't be ridiculous. Let me in'.

'I'm not letting a stranger into my house'.

'I'm not a stranger. And it's not your house; it's the shed'.

'Go away, Angina'.

'You promised you'd never call me that name again. Swine'.

Her footsteps grew skinny in the dark as she went back into her house. I had no nightmares that night.

We often met in the garden: she leaving out the bins, me sauntering around eating the raspberries or chomping on some early apples. 'Nice morning', I would call out to her and duck back into my refuge before she had the chance to pick up another stone and throw it at me. Her aim was getting better every time. One of these days I wouldn't be so lucky.

I was listening to Dolly Parton, crooning over easy to the thin walls that she would *aaa aaa aaalways* love me when the door burst open. Angie came in and stood looking at me. 'The doctor says all this is normal. We just have to be patient and get used to it. Adjustment time he called it. These little pills will do you wonders'.

Anything for a quiet life and one little pill wasn't going to do much mischief.

I settled back into my ordinary world in the shed. But that isn't the full story. Even when my colourful little bird charmed the old woman, with their wheelie shopping bags, from the other side of the street, and my chambers were now working beautifully, the pipes all connected and up and running, I still longed for something I had never tasted before.

Angie was a wise woman. Born old. Her mother popped her out of her own fifty-year-old body and the egg that met up with the jubilant swimming sperm of Angie's father was already half a century when it formed its unique little Angie zygote. She was always one-step ahead of me and when she arrived at the door with a big bowl of mangolds that was enough to coax me out of the shed and back into the house. Soon she had pots of swedes and floury balls of spuds boiling on the cooker all day long until the wallpaper began to peel away from the walls and fold down over the furniture. I lapped up each plateful that I had mixed with a good handful of bran. I was in my element putting on weight and believing that the past was in front of me and the future was all behind.

She decided we needed a holiday. A change of scene was what Doctor Angina ordered. 'There's nothing better than a cruise', she proclaimed. I couldn't think of anything worse. All those pea-green waves surging around me, waiting to swallow me whole and come back for my shadow while I had to look at the smug face of the Captain and the bloated stomachs of the passengers heaving from one over-stuffed buffet to the next.

I started to chew the inside of my jaw. Angina put her hands to her ears and ran into the next room. I rushed after her. Let me tell you that the noises I make when I chew the inside of my jaw are worse than chalk on a blackboard. Show me a woman that can put up with that sound and I will show you a man with four legs. It was only a matter of time before she caved in.

No cruise. No bingo. No karaoke. I had a hankering for woodland, moss, a carpet of mulched leaves damply rolled back to the earth. The mere thought of it and I could sniff out the loam in the under belly of trees. She pulled up websites, one after another. The south of France. Ho, ha, that's what I wanted, a gîte with a pond, men playing *boules* in the square. Kir Royales.

It had just rained a few days before we arrived and the air was hot and humid. We sat in cafés and drank red wine and sampled little dishes of delicacies. We wiped the sweat from our hot brows. We had to leave the windows open at night to let the air circulate through the room. I couldn't sleep.

The scent was very faint at first. It came in on the night air, circulated through the room so that I tossed and turned while Angina snored fartily beside me. In the morning I was haggard and worn out and walked through the house searching out the odour that was driving me to distraction. There was nothing for it but to go to a forest. An oak forest that was cool and welcoming.

My oh-so-wifely wife was in her power-walking mode and I let her off ahead of me. It was there under an all-embracing oak tree that it came upon me. The urge; the twitch of my nose as the scent came up to meet me. The need to snaffle the carpet of leaves away from the spot was so overwhelming that there was nothing for it but to go down on my hands and knees. I could smell the rain of ten days earlier, I could smell worms, leatherjackets, acorns and grubs somewhere in there, too. I put my nose right into it and started snouting around. This was what I was ordained to do. To find what was under the dark world and bring it into the light.

Up to this I never even liked soil under my nails. But here I was digging my hands right into it and the dark earth flew up into the air as if it were a black cloud of starlings. Oops, there I went again digging with the hunger sauce of what was underneath. A great sauce indeed, hidden from the eyes of woodlanders as they strolled through the leafy paths. As the scent grew stronger I got so excited I could hardly restrain myself. Near the roots of this particularly fine oak, its rope roots bulging from the earth, was my prize. Joy of joys, I lifted it out with the reverence of one lifting a newborn baby from its cradle. I pulled at my shirt-tail and carefully brushed the dirt from it. I stood back admiring the black treasure and was just about to open my mouth to experience my first gourmand's bite.

'Oh, no, you don't'.

Angina had come galumphing back and wrested it from my hands.

My new heart sank at the realisation that this could be taken from me.

'It's mine', I croaked, saliva running down my chin. I went to grab it from her. For a big woman she could move fast.

'Where did you get this?' she demanded holding up my prize fungus, her eyes bigger than I had ever seen before.

I brushed the smutch from my nose. The scent was so overwhelming that I could hardly breathe. I put my hand to my chest and tried to contain the urge to bite the fingers that held the jewel.

'Can I have it back?' I begged, my breath coming in short pants.

'Not now. Not when all heaven is breaking loose. A truffle this size is worth a fortune; must weigh a kilo at least. Any chef worth his condiment would kill to have it on his menu.

'You mean I can't eat it?' I cried.

She ignored my pleas as she started to root around in the bottom of her handbag, searching. 'How about some of that nice nougat we bought in the *confiserie* yesterday. It'll help your sugar levels', she said, 'before you get that nose down again'. Stuffing the sweets into my mouth, she unhooked the long, leather strap from her handbag. In the blink of her slippery, dippery eye she had me noosed with it.

'Now that you've been given the heart for foraging, it looks like it'll pay a fine dividend by the time I'm finished with you'.

That's what she thought.

Once Bitten

He told his secretary that he had a meeting across town; that it wouldn't be worth his while coming back to the office for the afternoon so she could leave early herself if she wished to avoid the Friday traffic. He hurried down the stairs and out into the afternoon, shading his eyes from the sun that was already half way to its own death.

He walked along the canal, by redbrick houses, steps leading up to solid doors and fanlights, by the park where forsythia was beginning to curl out some yolk-yellow through the rusted bars of the railings.

The hotel was busy, people booking in for the weekend. Wheelie bags and suitcases piled themselves up at the desk, waiting for the porter to bring them to their designated rooms. They knew him at reception by now; how close proximity to the street didn't appeal to him, so they gave him a room at the back that was quieter, unobtrusive. He signed in, then took the lift to the third floor, placed the card against the red light on the door handle until it clicked green and opened.

It was like all the other hotel rooms in all the other hotels across the city, with its heavy wine drapes and vertical blinds, sirens far off; seagulls sounding inland. He pulled off his jacket, his tie, slipped off his shoes and lay flat on the kingside bed. Narrow filaments of light spread across the bedclothes.

He rang for room service: a glass of Rioja, a panini with a little salad that he placed on the bedside locker. Turned the sign to 'do not disturb' on the door. He lay back on the white pillow with foam that was willing to hold the memory of him, but that was not what he wanted. No ghosts here. Not even a whisper of one. He took out some white sheets of paper from his laptop case, balanced them on the leather and started writing. He wrote until the light from the courtyard outside began to fade and he had to switch on the bedside lamp. He wrote three pages, A4 paper, a black pen. He prided himself on his ability to write in straight lines as if he had a ruler beneath his finger tips.

He wrote little things, letting out the dark that was inside him. Like how the condensation stayed on the window long after the room had warmed up, the robustness of the wine, the yellow flowers he saw on his way. He was careful not to expose too much, of where he lived, of where he went to work, though she already knew he was in accountancy and she had no problem telling him then that she was an interior designer of apartment blocks, old houses. He guessed from what she said that much of that line of work had dried up now.

He wanted to tell her that every man should plant a tree; every man should build a boat. All it would take was to buy the oak laths, steam them until they were supple enough to be curved into the vessel's ribs, covered in fibreglass, sealed. Then he could sail away when his soul was being taken from him.

But he held back.

He addressed the envelope, the PO Box number she had given him, the return address of the PO Box he had given her. It was the way it was. Nothing but the innocence of words. As clear and as clean could be.

Then it was time to fall through the body of himself and sleep came without objection, the taste of the Rioja still in his mouth, sharp, hot and dusty. Nothing disturbed him, not the words he held beneath his skin, not the wind that whipped up and battered against the walls, or the sirens screeching in far-off streets and the clink-clank of the Luas as it shunted by.

He woke an hour later, dressed, slipped into his shoes and made his way towards the train station and the start of the weekend. He thought about the animal that never took the same trail twice. This way made him easy. Home by another route.

All through Stephen's Green the paths were dry, ordered, no unruly weeds or walkways littered with leaves; beds all neat with cheeky primulas and wallflowers. It felt like he was in a foreign country, this tidiness. The afternoon of sleep and letter had turned him into someone else. He was a different man entering Grafton Street where the buskers were packing away their amps, spilling their day's takings into plastic bags. Down-and-outs loped towards no place.

He wandered into shops, through the loneliness in the rails of badly-cut garments. People rushing from one to another, purchases of last minute shopping, queuing to try on jeans that were too narrow at the knees, skinny legs, skinny legs where have you been. He wouldn't let any of that touch him, not even the child who was running in and out through the rails of clothes.

The station was an ant hive of disrupt, bodies flapping here and there for the last train. He looked out the window as the locomotive trundled out of the station. Out into the suburbs, away from the smoke and the fumes, the constant reminders. People's secrets piled up in their back yards that they let the commuters gawk at every day. Home was a four-bedroom detached in a cul-de-sac, the trees all darkness, a light burning in the porch, a door between him and his life behind it.

He waited a week before he went back to the post office. Lunchbreak and he turned the key on the box with his number on it, picked up her reply and put it in the inside pocket of his jacket. All her other replies were still there. At the back of the box. Hidden. Touching no other part of his life. No one getting hurt.

This latest one nestled against his chest like a warm bird, kept safe there until he got a chance to ring the hotel and book a room for the afternoon. A nod to his secretary, next day, a sub-group meeting he had to go to, would work from home later, and he returned to the security of an empty room, the bed-linen turned down, bleached of others' wrongdoing, a chocolate on the pillow.

When he was sixteen he had gone to France for the summer, picking grapes. He was a spotty boy-man with nothing but a notion that he would learn to love women and to be loved by them in return. He spent all day plucking fruit from the vines. Work of human hands in the heat of the sun. The cook in the kitchen at the back of the vineyard collected the bruised fruit from him and fed it to the chickens. The birds loved it and came running on their matchstick legs when she called them clucking and scratching to peck up every piece of dulcet flesh. They rewarded her by laying eggs that made good money for her, for they tasted of syllabub and were prized in the market and restaurants, were fought over by all the housewives of the region.

By evening his face had turned pink from the sun, his back stiff like an old man. The pickers all sat at big trestle tables for their dinner, platters of fatty meat and baguettes, ratatouille, wine harsh on his un-experienced tongue. But all that physical work had shaped his body. The sun had bleached his hair and the smell of acne disappeared from his skin. The egg woman took a fancy to him and coaxed him to the barn where he spilled all over her as soon as she touched him.

He took the letter from his pocket and held it to his cheek before he opened it. He had written that her words meant everything to him. She had replied that they were dust on the ground, a devalued currency. They could not keep the floods from the door, the fire from the upstairs window. Words would never call the man disconsolate from the roof. Inside every man was a stone, and inside the stone a word, a word that he carried all his life waiting for the stone to crack and let the word out.

He should let it out.

She had come back again into his life, thirty years on, through a college reunion. He didn't know what possessed him to go. Curiosity mainly, a little pride that he had not gone under, no scandal attached to him, a wife, a son, two daughters, still keeping his bills paid. Still a good head of hair. He recognised very few of the people that stood around laughing and clutching their glasses. A laugh that he thought way back then was endearing had turned into an irritating whine. There were names he would have stood up in court and swore he had never heard in his life as well as faces that he would have declared had never darkened the door of the university.

He didn't expect to see her there. She called out his name and he got a shock to see her so much the same and so much different all at once. Last time he heard of her she was breaking through the glass ceiling in Toronto. What had brought her back? As the evening wore on she could tell him things that were so far hidden in his mind that no archeologist would ever excavate them. Others were just under the surface waiting to be brought up for air.

She asked for his email address when others were passing around their business cards or punching numbers into their smart phones with alacrity. He declined. No phone number either. He had heard too many times how that ended up. No going there. But he knew where she worked.

A week later he could not resist the urge and found himself on the familiar street, passed the office with the name she had spoken of with some pride. He timed it well.

She came out at lunchtime and walked towards a wine bar that was further along the street. He followed her, slipped into the pub opposite and ordered a sandwich, a cup of coffee that was so bad he thought he was back in pre-ground bean days. The seat by the window gave him a good view of people wandering in and out and what he was watching for. When she came out at a few minutes before two, he bunched his napkin on the table and went towards her.

'What a coincidence', she had said, without surprise when she saw him. As if she had been expecting it all the time. 'Not seeing one another in thirty years and then twice in one week. It must be fate', she smiled.

A meeting on the hurried street, he turning to go back to work and she touching his shirt sleeve. They painted masterpieces of such encounters.

He had a wife, he had children, grown up but still a financial burden, not out on their own, not able to fend for themselves, still cubs in the den waiting for the food to be brought back to them, still waiting for the money to come as if he were a walking ATM machine. They would always come first. He walked away from her, the heat of her hand still burning through his shirt. He felt his heart had wings, 'imped' like a bird the falconer grafted extra feathers onto to make it fly better.

Later when he took the shirt off he held it to his face momentarily. He could follow her scent from it though there was no trace of perfume. He bundled it in the laundry basket and when he showered he held his hand outside the plastic curtain where the water splashed on the blue and white fish.

Worse than a teenager.

He sat with his wife at dinner. They talked as they always did about their day and the little exigencies of life that could make things difficult to bear if there wasn't the companionship of someone to be coming home to. They watched the news together. More austerity measures across the board. She laughed and consoled him. At least they weren't being strangled by a mortgage. They were nearly out the other end with theirs; they could pay it off in the morning if they wanted to. Maybe they should do that. Pay it and be done with it. Then just take off. Rent a cave in Ibiza, be the hippies they never gave themselves the chance to be. Down to the beach every day, the water howlite blue, a lagoon deep enough to keep her afloat, sun ripples on the water, a short walk to the bar, mint macerated with sugar, dissolving in the clear viscous liquid. Olives, salty anchoas, bread to mop up the oil.

'Dream that', his wife told him. She was his rock. Nothing would ever change that. He let her go to bed before him.

How an innocuous sentence could unhinge his day. Was it possible that he had something to give? All this energy that it took to live an ordinary life, when there were miracles inside never getting the chance to throw their crutches by the side of the grotto. She had penned that.

So much to want.

'However, we could never meet up', he had written.

'There is no room in a real life for the word "however". It is a word that carries snakes in its pocket', she replied.

The heart never lets go. It holds down in there between the breath and the stopping of it. There is only the breath in the end until it is gone.

Second year arts. She had come and kissed his neck while he was sitting in the library trying to work out why Alexander the Great was so great. The kiss went right down through his body until he grew big with want. He saw her again later in the lecture hall chatting to the girl in the row in front of him. She looked up and smiled when the lecture was over before walking up the steps and out of the hall. He watched for her every day just to get a smile and when she didn't appear one Tuesday at lectures he asked her friend where she was. She was in bed with the 'flu.

He scribbled her address on the edge of his jotter and skipped the last lecture before lunch to take the bus northside. He followed the paths by lonely, grey houses until he found one with a dozen bins spilling out onto the pavement. Her bedsit was on the top floor. A man with no shirt on let him into a dark hallway with bicycles leaning against the banisters. Someone's transistor was on in the downstairs room and there was the hiss and spit of frying coming from a half-open door.

He found her room and knocked. There was no answer so he pushed in the unlatched door. The curtains were closed, there was the smell of Vicks and the one-bar electric heater glowed towards the bed where she lay. The air was stifling. He touched her forehead. That heat, the feverish heat of her body in a room where the walls were bare and rows of mouldy teacups were scattered on chairs and shelves, textbooks opened, their covers torn and ragged. He called her name a few times before she opened her eyes.

She was burning up.

He brought her down the corridor to the communal bathroom and filled the tub with tepid water, then helped her into it. He watched over her until she began to shiver. He helped her out of her wet t-shirt and wrapped her in a towel then half-walked, half-carried her back to her bed. He lay down beside her in the narrow single space with sheets that were damp from sweat and bath water. He looked up at the polystyrene tiles that were falling off the ceiling, all the time grateful to be there looking at them.

He lay with her that evening smelling the strong heat and sweat off her body burning towards him. He forgot afternoon lectures, the play he was to go to with friends that evening. He got up to make some tea and found an opened pack of digestives which he took onto a tiny balcony overlooking the back gardens of other houses. In between the washing lines, junk piles of slates and barrels, a black cat and her two kittens played in the long grass climbing on to the rusted, corrugated roof and tight-roped across the thin edge of the wooden fence.

Early in the morning her fever broke. He woke to find her eyes looking at him. Then she pressed him hard to her, kissed him until his mouth ripened, then kissed him again until he opened for the swollen tongue that was his. Tiny explosions, fireworks, filled every cell of his body. So this is what it's like, this is what it's all about, he thought. He curled his arms around her waist, holding her to him as his hands found her. Not afraid to cry out, not afraid to let the occupants of the other flats hear his mouth swollen for her, sucking her in like the soft fruit sitting in the bowl on the table.

He didn't know who he was then. Life came rushing in at him and he felt himself open like a shell, a scallop or a mussel clinging to a rock that filtered all the goodness flowing towards him as the tide came in to cover him.

Two days later he saw her in the queue in the cafeteria, placing a plate of curried chips onto a tray, laughing with the guy beside her who wrapped his woollen scarf around her neck. He sat in the lecture hall, trying to concentrate on how Alexander came through the pass of Thermopylae.

Did it ever happen, did he ever go to her room; did he ever lie in her fevered bed and know himself like he had never known before?

However.

Nevertheless.

Yet.

After all these years, she was challenging him, telling him that word was a snake in the pocket. But a whole house could crumble on the one word breaking from the stone within him.

He took out the pen and paper. He wrote that he wouldn't be contacting her again. That such foolishness had no future and she was not to reply. 'Sometimes we have to fight very hard to keep what we have', he concluded. He sealed the envelope and put it in his case, reminding himself that he would get it in the last post box before the train station. Then he lets his eyes close. He slept the sleep of the unencumbered, thinking of the lines that she has written. *Let all your words be birds in flight.*

He slept on and on. He didn't hear the lift clatter up and down the space beyond his room or the door cling-cling, open, footsteps gather all along the corridor. Revellers coming back from the bar after a team-building meeting, laughing and calling at doors to be let in caused him no disturbance. Somewhere from the suitcase of dream, worlds toppled over, things spilled out, full of loves and bare breasts, his throat, the tender areas of his heart that he had never exposed.

When he woke the room was in darkness. A voice in the wind knocked against the wall and pecked and pecked at the windowpane demanding to get in, asking him how he had arrived at this season of failed fire. He jumped up from the bed and dressed as quickly as he could.

He ran along the street as if the pavement was scorching the soles of his feet. Stars splintered into fragments, fell faster than light. His coat flapped against the bruised sky and brazier of moon. But he knew it is too late: The last train home already moving out of the station, the seed of a lie forming.

Pretty Bird, Why You So Sad?

We were out cutting wood. Greg had the chainsaw going full throttle and me feeding him the logs, careful with my fingers, sawdust peppering my boots when we heard the gas guzzler pull into the yard. Greg switched off the machine, I whipped off my gauntlets. We were ready for a break anyway. The smell of resin hung in the air.

We're used to locals dropping in for a 'squawk gawk' as Greg calls it, but this jeep wasn't from around here. Its big, shiny door opened and two legs swung themselves out. Spit-polished shoes placed themselves on the gravel; a head emerged before the belly released every bit of itself from the driver's seat, bespoke suit straining at its seams. You know the sort of bucko I'm talking about, from a two-up two-down, made his money in red diesel, angel dust. Not afraid to leave his footprints on your back as he climbs over you to get to where he wants.

'Out you come, Li', he said.

I watched as a young woman crept out from the passenger seat, sleeked, jet hair framing a pretty face with almond eyes that had the light switched off in them. She peered up at him, waiting for a crumb of kindness from his lips. You'd be anxious for her that she might fall frozen from a tree without complaining.

'I'll have one of your birds', Your Man said to Greg ignoring me since I'm at the age when women are invisible anyway. 'Something to jizz this one up a bit. Take the long face of misery off her'.

We're not in the habit of selling our birds. We work hard to keep them in good fettle, making sure they're free from disease; fit them out with climbing nets, full spectrum lamps to brighten the grey, drizzly days we get around here. Greg is fierce choosy about the branches he cuts for them, nice and shapely, with bark good enough to sharpen their beaks on, or to clutch all shape and size of claw.

So Greg told him as much.

'You'll let us have a look at them, at least', Your Man said, 'Li here wants to see them. Don't you, petal?'

The young woman nodded.

'No harm in that', Greg responded.

Around the back of the house we went, Your Man going on and on about the houses he still owned, the one in the Algarve that was too good to get rid of and the estate he'd finish as soon as the banks started moving again.

There was the ruction of feather and wing as we came close to the aviary, chirping and screeching when Greg whistled to them. They love to see us coming, calling the morning into existence in their big, full-throated song, their colours shouting at one another: the Rainbow Lorikeet with its orange jacket, the Blue-Fronted Amazon, the Sulphur-Crested Cockatoo with a fine, sunny head on it. I couldn't take my eyes off Li's sad face as she stood there, looking at them. She put out her hand and touched the wire mesh. It was as if she was the one behind bars, dreaming of what it would be like out there among the birds in the lush foliage of jungle.

A little smile appeared around her eyes when Charlie squawked at her to 'open the door', 'open the door'. She moved along, standing for a while in front of the Golden Oriole. She then stopped beside a pair of the African parrots that were caressing each other with their bills.

'You can see why they're called lovebirds', Greg said, turning towards her.

'Wouldn't you like a little lovebird', Your Man simpered, and rubbed his big nose against hers in imitation. I wanted to reach out and thump him in the face.

'No', she said quietly. 'This one'.

Compared to all the others, the bird she was pointing to was not the sort that'd catch your eye, even on a bad day. It had the look of a creature that might have been bright once but somehow its colour had been washed away by roosting too long in the rain, leaving it with a grey tail and beak, dull, brown wing and crown as it pecked away on the bark of the branch.

The more Li looked at it, the more I saw the change come over her; a light entering her eyes, sadness dissolving as it slowly began to slip down her cheeks, down her shoulders, melt into the ground. Our Vinous-throated Parrot-bill had switched on the sun inside her.

Your Man put his thick fingers into his pocket and pulled out a wodge of money.

'How much?' he insisted.

'They're not for selling', Greg replied.

'This pile of money would buy you ten birds better than that. In this climate only a three-quarters eejit would turn that down'.

Greg O'Halloran wasn't for budging and gave him as good as he got. Listening to Your Man argue, you could see how easily he'd get an incinerator built beside a crèche, a housing estate on a flood plain, a road through a ring fort. We were standing there, Greg about to head back to his sawing when I looked at the little one opposite me, her head down, her shoulders tight.

A tear fell.

I pucked Greg in the ribs with my elbow: 'Let her have it'. It galled him, but that's one thing I'd say about him. There's a soft bit somewhere deep inside him and he can't see bird nor human in pain.

'You won't always get your own way, you know', he said to Your Man as he put the money in his leather gauntlet.

'Want a bet?'

Greg turned on his heels and headed back to the saw horse.

The smell of Your Man's money was in the house long after his four-wheel drive had hit the dust. I opened all the windows to let the clean air in. Mrs Nolan came for her free range eggs. What with the Orpingtons and the Rhode Islands, we had a good few layers, and I had my regular customers. They kept coming back saying that they hadn't seen glair that clear or a yolk that yellow since they were children. Mrs Nolan swore by them for her sponges. She wanted to enter another for the Agricultural Fair because the last time she won a rosette for a cake the judge said it was the colour of heaven. She made the front page of the local paper.

'Who owned the fancy jeep', she wanted to know as she stood at the door with her dozen gugs.

'Just another squawk-gawker', I misinformed her.

While Greg was on his nightly walk around the birds, I switched on the news and gave my hands a bit of a pamper. They were showing their age, a dead giveaway. I lathered them with the moisturiser that our Betsy brought me the last time she came. I covered each of them with a plastic bag, sealed it with masking tape to get the full effect and, just like Cleopatra, let my poor, wrinkled skin drink in the milk and honey lotion. Then I broke into the HobNobs, feeling like a snake with its forked tongue, letting the bird go like that, thinking what I'd do with the money.

I was in the market the following week checking out the egg competition: duck eggs, big blue goose eggs, free range from down the country. Greg likes that nice sausage the Germans sell so I headed towards it, my tongue already tasting its garlicky pig smell as I walked along by the railings of St Nick's. It was making heavy rain and people nearly took the eye out of me with their umbrellas, me weaving in and out trying to avoid the drips that fell from canopies. I wandered past the woman who sells the gorgeous painted glass, past the organic vegetable sellers, big heavy loaves of sourdough. Li was standing behind her stall with its array of silk handkerchiefs and ties, two men quizzing her if they were the real thing, she showing them the label. The taller of the two bought one with a saxophone streaming down the length of fabric, the other chose one covered in guitars. I went to go towards her but she caught my eye, shook her head, looked down into her biscuit tin of cash and started counting coins. She then busied herself with the burden of straightening the ties as soon as the men left with their purchases.

I headed back towards the corner and there was Your Man himself, at the gate of the school, one eye on her, his phone growing out of his ear as he bulldozed through a deal with whoever was at the other end. Letting on I was buying lettuce plants, I watched him flip-close his phone and head across the road towards her, without looking, cars pulling to a halt, Moses with the sea parting before him. All I could see was him bending over her and his hand jabbing her shoulder about something or other that she had done wrong. With that he moved through the crowds, slapping shoulders with his newspaper, shaking off the rain as he entered the coffee shop further up.

A week later, Greg had gone off to a REPS meeting in the community centre and I was getting one of the Silver-Spangled Hamburgs ready for the show. It had been washed, dried, its feathers all glossy from the pellets Greg had been feeding it. I was just putting Vaseline on its comb to bring up the colour when I caught a movement out of the corner of my eye making its way up the path. It took me a minute to make out the shape. It was Li, burdened by the cage in her hand. I took it from her and brought her into the kitchen. I wasn't sure what she was saying as she tried to explain, moving her elbows back and forth to indicate what had happened.

The gist of it was that the bird never settled; as soon as she took it home it started to fret, barely took a bite, flying around and around, bashing itself against the wire sides trying to get out. I could see it was in a sorry state. Its feathers were dull, dishevelled looking with a bald patch on its chest where it was stress-preening as Greg calls it. We would have our work cut out for ourselves if we wanted to hold onto it.

She was crying softly by now. She couldn't bear to see the pretty bird so sad. I stroked her hair telling her that everything would be fine, smoothing its black silkiness until she felt secure enough to tell me how she had come to Ireland three years before. Your Man had got her a good job in the Saturday market and a room in a fancy house.

She had a little boy back home; she couldn't lose her job. She needed it to send money back for him and her mother who was looking after him. He was seven. She took out her phone and showed me a picture of him. A beautiful boy.

My old heart cried for her.

I knew where she lived sure enough, nothing fancy about that, in the outskirts, houses boarded up, bins outside for days, dirty nappies trapped in the corners of rotting fencing. She had the upstairs room and shared the kitchen with six others. Your Man said that if she caused him no trouble he would bring her son and her mother over too.

Together we concocted the story she would tell him. How she had been cleaning out the cage and the Parrot-bill saw the open window. How she couldn't catch him but saw him fly over the rooftops, the church spire, up into the open space of the sky. I took her by the hand and we went outside with the cage. I opened the gate and placed it on the floor of the aviary. We opened the little wire door. We stood back, waited, biding our time.

When we had all but given up, it gave a little hop and then another, out onto the floor of the enclosure. It looked around as if taking it all in, remembering, and then it flew up into one of the fancy new perches Greg had just bought. It started to preen almost straight away.

FEEDING THE WOLF OF LIES

All through the day the geckos come, flicking up the walls, their tails writing dark all over the plaster. They turn, their black, unmoving eyes stare at Margaret and in them she sees the faces of long-forgotten lovers – Simon whom she had fallen for first, in the way a girl-woman loves, not knowing clearly what love is; Tom Oakes as strong and solid as his name and so rooted in his own world she could never shift him from his own spot; David, with his dark hair, his musky smell, his cruel hands, and a miscarriage that she was always grateful for. A necklace of tongues whispering round her neck: Bitch, Bitch. But no curses from the one who haunts her, the one she deserves lacerations from.

The curtain is a wild animal trying to get out, lifting its hooves over the windowsill in an attempt to escape into the courtyards and beyond that the Sierras. 'Go back, go back', its eyes flare but there is no way of finding the way back now.

Voices filter through the fever and when her mind isn't a burning bush in the corner of the room she can make out shapes at the end of the bed calling her. A wet compress is placed on her forehead but she pushes it away because it weighs on her like a barrel of stones. Slipping, slipping. She is slipping down into the bowels of the bed.

'Pull me up, pull me up'.

'Shhh', is all that Carmina says and rubs her forehead again. 'Cristobal is coming, he will be here soon'.

The man who comes and sits by her side is not the one who haunts her.

All these years fighting with the two wolves inside her: the one that was truth, the one that was lies. Starving the first; feeding the latter all this time until it has grown so fat it has swollen like an egg inside her. If she could just step through the fire, a Joan of Arc, then she would be ...

But she is falling, falling.

Carmina stuffs the keyholes with fennel seed to keep out the fever, but all it does is block the cooling breeze that wants to come to her as does the moon, lazy on its back or bright pieces of stars. She has no cure nor has the doctor with his medicine show in the market place, his two iguanas in the crate beside him. He sways Carmina so easily with his sleight of hand. He lifts them out, their tails swishing back and forth as he proclaims to the widening circle how his tincture, made of their very special fat, will cure everything. He demonstrates, draws blood with a knife borrowed from the fishmonger's stall, and, hey presto, he is miraculously healed by the brown tincture he pours on it. A bargain, at two bottles for ten euro. Carmina comes running back with its surety, pouring it on a spoon and then to Margaret's lips. She cannot bear it; she dry retches at the mere smell of it.

No iguana fat will cure her.

She can only take little sips of water, though her mouth is parched for it and she cries out to have it quenched. A little sliver of persimmon, maybe, or some melon that she can feel cool on her lips; let its smoothness slip down her throat and stamp out the fire that's raging inside her body. Her very bones are being singed, starting with her feet that are two furnaces; as if Carmina has brought in the winter *bracero* filled with glowing coals and puts it to the soles of her feet, scorching the thin skin first, then flesh. Her feet will burn away until they are ash, then it will be her ankles, her shins, knees, femur, hip-bone all the way up along her spine, disc by spongy disc and as the fire rages through her no water can put it out, no pineapple juice nor Doctor One Bottle's tincture nor the prayers of Fr Lopez.

Husk. Chaff. Nothing inside her to hold herself together any more. How careless she had been with the happiness she once wore. She had taken it off like she would a precious necklace and left it unattended on the window sill. She turned her back on it and didn't see the magpie that came in through the open pane, picked up her world in its beak and brought it back to its nest; tore it apart like it would a song bird. Pitiless. It shredded all those little bits of laughter, soft touchings of a child's face, an evening at the bog and pushed them into the stolen gatherings of its roost. It grackled at the good of it, the way her happiness made the place warmer for its own scrawny chicks, that only weeks before were mere yolk and glair.

She had grown up knowing the way farmers around the village back home learned how to kill a pig. The only way was by doing it, sticking a knife in its heart, bleeding it out all over the ground. It was the same with going. There was no other way.

Now she has to remember, to pass everything back through the heart. So she starts where it started for her with the brown moth beating its wings on the windowpane trying its damndest to get out. When she saw it trapped there she had got up from the breakfast table, opened the window and set it free. After the girls had gone to school, she pulled her coat from the hook behind the door. The radio told her that rain was spreading to the rest of the country, but in that little patch there was still some coinage of blue, a glint of sun on the stripped trees. She slipped from the house, closing the door behind her, the cat waiting for an opening so it could slide in and curl under the range. Margaret wished she had the gifts of the cat: to be able to walk about in dark and in light, to be able to keep her feet from getting wet, but most of all to be able to forget.

She gave a small wave to Bernard as he worked on repairing the gate into the Black Meadow. He looked up from what he was doing and waved back – an uneasy wave of one who didn't know how to deal with her any more. She could feel his eyes watching her as she walked out the yard. A sparrow hawk sat on a branch listening to the false call of the thrush pretending she was his mate.

She continued away from him, the scarf keeping her unruly hair in check. She followed the old road, past fields waiting for winter.

'The life you save may not even be your own', she heard a voice from the bushes. She looked around to see who was talking, but there was no one. She walked as far as the crossroads where the mark of the bone-fire was still a black spool on the road. She walked, her head down, looking at the weeds that grew along the middle. Daisies and self-heal and plantain had found a place to root and were willing to settle for it.

Bernard was still in the same place as she came back into the yard, her face held up to the sun that was shining through the clouds. She came towards him, touched the sleeve of his jumper. He turned from his task and she could see the pain on his face.

'Are you ok?' she asked him.

'What has been taken from us?' he said, his voice wavering. She feared he might cry and she couldn't bear that. It would break her altogether to see tears in his eyes, for it was too late now.

'My heart lifted as soon as I saw you walking back the lane', he continued. She could feel the strength of his arm against her fingers and she left it there momentarily.

'You must be famished with the hunger', she said so kindly she almost changed her mind. 'Why don't I make us a boiled egg, and we'll have it before the girls come home from school?' She looked up at him and knew what he saw in her face and what he believed he saw were two different things.

While she was clearing away the dishes she broached the subject. A day or two was all she asked. Just for herself. Dublin, maybe. It would give them a bit of space away from one another; help clear the troubles between them. Mrs King could help out with the girls. She would go ask her later on.

He said 'yes'. She knew he would give her anything if he thought it would cleave her to him.

What was she to make of that day she went, the hare across her line of vision, the skulk of foxes? She had brought the bin down to the end of the lane, waiting for the bin men. The road beckoned to her saying, 'see where I can bring you'. She could smell the sleep of duvets as she walked by houses, the cow that still cried for the calf that was taken from her. She walked as far as the town. Lorries were pulled up in loading bays delivering milk and bread. The man carried the tray of fresh-sliced pans into the shop and she stole a small loaf while his back was turned. She pulled at the heel of the bread, smelling of lunchboxes and schoolbags. It nearly stopped her in her tracks.

But it didn't.

She took the train to Dublin.

She found herself able to breathe as soon as the carriages swung out of the station and headed east. She walked along the street, people all hustly-bustly as Mrs King described it after her first and only visit there. She looked up at the GPO, the world moving towards her and away from her at the same time.

She took the bus to the Botanic Gardens.

She wandered by the meticulous flowerbeds, under the great canopy of the trees and found her way to the glass conservatories. All day her eyes could find no rest among the beautiful flowers, even the slipper orchids that wanted to give themselves to her. She touched the soft petals. But they didn't settle her.

Her first thought, when she saw Cristobal standing at the other end of the glasshouse, in front of one of the orchids she had earlier admired, was that she would have to stand on her toes to reach his mouth and suck the sweet flesh of it. She turned to the window as if taking in the sun. There was no one else in the conservatory. The air was musk and heat and there was a man smiling down at her, words spilling around her, swamping her.

'You look so much like me', he had said to her. 'You have the same mouth, the same wicked mouth'. His words didn't startle her because she recognised herself in what he said, for there was just the two of them and it was so natural to talk about the fire that burned between them.

A shaft of sun came in through the glass of the conservatory. His voice started to melt the frozen parts of her heart and it made her feel like one of the rare flowers in the glasshouse that opened its gold-green sepals first, then unfurled its petal lips sending out its hot scent, its tempted colour. He told her of his life where the blue of the sky met the scent of orange blossom along the street.

She moved towards him.

And while she was talking to him she didn't once think of her own life. That belonged to someone else now.

The lie.

How easily it came to her. It sounded so intensely believable, she convinced even herself. She blocked out the wet dog scraping at the door trying to get in, the girls doing lessons at the table, overalls on the back of the chair, crows on the backs of the cows picking the ordinary nuisances from their hides. He pulled back her hair and she drank in the clean citrus smell of him. They walked the length of the street to the hotel where he stayed every time he came to the city and where the receptionist was always discreet.

He poured her a glass of wine, he loosened his tie. Then he undid each button at the back of her wool dress and she shivered as she felt his fingers touch her skin. He slipped the dress from her shoulders and placed his face to the small of her back like a man who had been in a desert for weeks, had found an oasis and could now drink his fill. She let him crush her body to his heat, her own thirst knowing how it could be sated.

Afterwards, while she listened to him sleeping evenly beside her she knew that he had released something in her, something that she did not even know she had imprisoned. Something that was almost impossible to comprehend when she heard herself cry out. She could feel her tears fall on the fine cotton pillows.

She had gone looking for this. She had opened the door behind which she kept secrets, the secrets she did not even share with herself and let this happen. The thread which had bound her to Bernard had been unravelling all this time and there was nothing to clutch onto any more. They had eked out their pinched existence and what was there to keep them together now that she had heard the cry inside her?

She and Bernard were broken and there was no way of ever fixing them again. All she had to do was close that door on her life with him and her children and put the dog of all forgetfulness in front of it. Give the animal a jowl big enough, a bark loud enough, and any attempt to ever go near that door again would be stopped by its bared teeth. The more she did that the more she believed in her own lies. She reached out for Christobal's hand and put it on her belly.

She was surprised at how easy it had been to slip into the skin of someone else as she stepped out into the new world of his home. She looked up at the cobalt windows against the white walls and, above that, bluer still, while all around her was the ripe scent of figs and morning sounds. Arms that tied her to herself now moved up and out like a dancer, her body unfurling to the draw of the heat.

She fed the wolf of lies.

Evening carries sounds to her, sounds of feet stomping the floor and the rhythm of hands clapping. Carmina hurries away to shush them while they beat out the music that is in their bones, their sinews, in the very haem of them; up there on the rooftop terrace where they gather in the evening's cooling time and swallows cut the air. She will never be part of them now. She climbed up to them once, hoping to sit with them. She stood there as they talked so fast that their letters melted at the ends of words like chocolate in the heat. They saw her but didn't invite her to sit. If she walked these courtyards till the sun became a cold spot in the sky she would never be one of them. She is and always was an *extranjera,* a foreigner. They passed the kachimbah around, drinking in the smoke from its pipe. Smoking away their own memories that they didn't want to remember again. Everyone had memories that they wanted to keep buried.

But it makes no difference now.

Many days she found herself on streets she didn't know. She walked by open doors letting in the breeze, the plants of the patios lush and cooling, women sitting at their doorways, gathered together in the evening light, to talk of days' work and their difficult husbands, their children far away. Sitting there in their housecoats – like her old neighbours that she left behind, Mrs King and Mrs Lynch – with their varicose legs stretched out in front of them, abscessed, gangrenous, one disfigured toe bent over the other as they opened their mouths and laughed in a language she was not party too and never would be. The memory pushed so far back into her past that she covered over with laughter and other useless things.

Thin, imperious cats walked in and out of shadows grabbing at life and followed her through the streets. Open doorways with bright geometric tiles and fronds of plants shivered in the light and from a cage within the patio came a most beautiful singing. A yellow bird poured out all its heart into the doorway and onto the street. She stood to hear it sing and it filled her with joy. She realised that it was everything to her, this singing. That the creature could sing even though it was caged. For being confined didn't prevent it from singing out to the world.

It kept her going for a long time.

She wakes. There are people in the room though she can't see them. She is dying. She calls out for her mother, calls to the bright light outstretched at the end of her bed. She scratches at the thin sheet that covers her body, searching in all its folds in the hope of finding her lost children that are hidden there. If she only looks hard enough. She can hear Cristobal's voice from somewhere beside her. Other voices too. Her body is letting go of that hell of heart that had been burning her up. All that way back when she flamed and the world around her caught fire and consumed her. Afterwards how everyone in the village and the other surrounding villages must have talked about her, bleeding out all kindness, all compassion for her. How could she do it; leave a good man like Bernard and her children.

Her children above all else. Her bloodline. No woman in her right mind. But they were young, resilient.

The next time Carmina comes into the room, she sits by the bed and takes Margaret's hands in hers. How broad they are, how generous and kind her fingers. Then she touches her forehead and Margaret feels the coolness there too. But she is afraid. What if the fire from her skin spreads to Carmina, catches her body too and rages through hers? She must try and speak before they are all consumed by it. What is important is that she can tell her own story. That she will find the strength to let them know her forgotten home before she goes.

She owes them that at least.

The evening before she finally left, she slipped from the bed and sat in the chair by the far corner. Whatever light was in the room came from the moon finding its way through the half-closed curtains. Somewhere outside an owl scanned the soot and white world below him, ready to pounce. Stars shone their dying light of a million years on the fields and trees. Light reflected on the mirror of the dressing table with her face creams and a brush holding the dark hairs from a child's head. She sat listening to the rise and fall of Bernard's breathing, watched the contour of his face, and she willed forgiveness into his heart. He had turned his body then and she held her breath for a second, afraid he would wake and find her there and he would know that within its shape of muscle and tissue her heart inhabited a different place.

She sat there trying to make him dream a dream of her that was not unkind. That he might let the little window in his mind open again into a field with horse-chestnut trees on that day stolen from summer when they were able to touch one another for a short while without it hurting.

She had told Cristobal that day in the Botanic Gardens that her husband was dead. Never blessed with children. Cristobal had believed her. What did she do but lock her family away as if they were convicts to be sent to the Tower of London? Packed into a room of little ease. Squeezing them smaller and smaller until their bones were crushed to ash even as she was burning up herself. By lying about her family she had denied their very existence. There was no one ever to ask about them. No one to ever say their names in her presence. She had denied them all those years but it was time to make recompense.

She must name them now.

She opens the well of her mouth to confess to Carmina. There is no sound. Nothing comes out.

She tries again.

Nothing.

Again.

Nothing.

The least she must do is call them by their names: Hansie, Carmel, Bernard. But they are so far down, at the bottom of the well, the cord that would have pulled the bucket up has snapped. There is no way of getting them out now. How easily she had played with them all her life? Thinking there was time to recompense. The wolf that was truth she has starved to death. The wolf that was lies has won.

Through the flames she can see fields of sunflowers, an

army of yellow pilgrim faces marching down the low hills. Olive trees in even rows, their silvery greenness quivers in the wind, throwing their shadows onto the farmer as he pull his mattock across the scorched earth.

ABOUT THE AUTHOR

Geraldine Mills is a poet and short story writer. She has published four collections of poetry, the first two, *Unearthing your Own* (2001) and *Toil the Dark Harvest* (2004) from Bradshaw Books. Arlen House published *An Urgency of Stars* (2010) for which she was awarded a Patrick and Katherine Kavanagh Fellowship. She collaborated with American poet, Lisa C. Taylor on the joint collection, *The Other Side of Longing* (Arlen House, 2011), which was chosen as the Gerson Reading at the University of Connecticut, 2011. Arlen House has published her first two short story collections, *Lick of the Lizard* (2005) and *The Weight of Feathers* (2007), for which she received an Arts Council Bursary.

Her prizes include the Penguin/RTÉ Guide Short Story Competition, the William Trevor Award, Fish Publishing Award, and the Francis MacManus Award. She was the millennium winner of the Hennessy/*Sunday Tribune* Emerging Fiction Award and the overall winner of the New Irish Writer Award for her story 'Lick of the Lizard'. Her fiction is taught on university contemporary literature courses in the USA, where she has facilitated workshops on the short story and poetry. Her work has been published in *The Sunday Tribune, The Irish Times, Poetry Ireland Review, The Atlanta Review, de brakke hond, Dog Days and Other Stories, The Stinging Fly* and *The SHOp*, among many others. It has also been broadcast on RTÉ and Lyric FM. She is a creative writing tutor with NUI Galway and is an on-line tutor with Creative Writing Ink where she teaches the Advanced Short Story Course.

www.geraldinemills.com